satan, is that you?

WELCOME TO HELL

BOOK 1

JANET LEE SMITH

Book Cover by ZoneArtz Design

Edited by: Kate Seger

This book is dedicated to the authors I've met over the past year. I never realized how valuable a community of authors could be.

CHAPTER ONE

well, hello there!

"HEY! How did you get into my office? Humans aren't supposed to be let in here without my prior permission. I don't believe you belong down here yet. Are you some reporter or something? Reporters think coming down here, meeting me, and checking things out is fun. So, what's your name?"

The stranger sat with one foot tapping on the floor as if nervous. He didn't look at me as he cast his eyes around the room. Once he finished looking around my office, his gaze fell on me. My body seemed to come alive as his eyes pinned me to my seat. What was going on? This was a new feeling for me.

He looked anxious, but he also held my gaze. The tension wasn't present in his eyes, but in his body language. While his foot continued to tap on the floor, he ran his hand through his hair. It was as if he didn't know what to do with himself. After what seemed like hours but was only a couple of minutes, he responded to me.

"My name is Jacob. Ummm, are you truly Satan?" When my publisher told me to go to Hell to interview Satan for a book he wanted me to write, I was confused. I never believed in Hell. Now I'm even more confused. If Hell exists, which it does, how is Satan a

1

female? Gideon has not only been my publisher for years, we've been friends since childhood. I couldn't help but wonder if this was all a joke on his part. Did he really want a book written about Hell?

Looking around the office, I realized that whoever decorated it had horrible taste. The walls were all painted white, which alone seemed weird for Satan's office. But what I really couldn't understand was how much pink was in the room. In one corner was a couch with matching chairs, all in pink, with throw pillows to match. Across from her desk was what amounted to a small kitchen area where there sat a pink microwave and coffee maker. It was like Pepto Bismol threw up in the place.

Once I finished looking around the office, my gaze fell on the woman I came to see. Once her eyes found mine, I couldn't look away from her. Earlier, when we shook hands, I felt an electric shock, and now, staring into her eyes, my breathing quickened. What did I find so fascinating about this woman?

"Oh, you're shocked. Most people are. People think I'm a dude, a scary-looking dude. Red skin, horns, hooves, and a tail. My brother and I did a fantastic job with our stories. People rarely believe the truth without seeing it with their own eyes or hearing the story from my brother and me."

I watched as this beautiful woman sat behind a massive mahogany desk and offered me the seat in front of it. She then reached into a drawer to grab something. *This is Satan, and I'm in Hell. You would think I would be afraid of whatever she pulls out of that drawer. But she is so gorgeous. That's all I can focus on.*

Long red, curly hair. The color of fire. That was ironic. Her green eyes were a beautiful shade of hunter green. That's always been my favorite hue of green. Her body was the shape of an hourglass, and her legs went on and on. She wore jeans so tight they looked like someone painted them on her and showed off her ass perfectly, and a turtleneck, so no cleavage showed. But that shirt showed off her breasts perfectly.

"Yo, Jacob, can you stop staring at me now? It's rude. I know how hot I am, but it's still rude to stare. Here, you're going to have to wear this. Put it around your neck."

Her hands brushed against mine as she handed me the laminated card hanging from a lanyard. A pink one. Did she really expect me to wear this? It only had the words "Satan's Guest" on it. Realizing I didn't have a choice, I placed it around my neck.

"You need to wear it the whole time you're down here. Without it, you'll be stopped by my guards. Just remember, we will read your book before it's published. If you write anything I don't like, you may find yourself here on a more permanent basis, if you know what I mean. I know people like to call me Satan, but my real name is Tempest.

"I am not a fallen angel. I jumped from Heaven because I wanted something different. If you tell anyone I said that, I'll deny it. God is my brother. I like to say he pushed me though the pearly gates because he hates it when I say that. He believes in the stories we created about us, Heaven, and Hell and likes to act holier than thou. He did want to push me because Lilith preferred me to him, but I didn't give him a chance, I jumped. That was a long fall, let me tell you. And it hurt. I broke almost every bone in my body."

Satan is a female named Tempest, and Lilith prefers Tempest to God. Is Satan, I mean Tempest, a lesbian? That would be a shame. That would mean I don't have a shot with her. Not that I think I have a shot with her, to begin with. Or that I want a shot with her. After all, she is Satan. But how much do I know about Satan? Not much, it would seem.

"You would think he would push Lilith since he wanted to push me, but no, he thought she was the love of his life and kept her up there. I wish I could have seen his face when she walked out of the pearly gates and jumped down. She jumped right into my domain and helped me build Hell along with the other Demons who jumped."

This conversation always brought back memories of that time, and it was never easy. My brother and I had our issues, but I loved him deeply and missed him on a daily basis. That was something I wouldn't admit to anyone. I needed to do something to get these thoughts out of my head, so I decided to make coffee before continuing. "Would you like a cup of coffee, Jacob?"

He shook his head no, still not taking his eyes off me. Was it possible he was feeling the same way I was? Since he was human, the chances were he wasn't. Perhaps it was surprise over me being a female. Once the coffee was done, I poured a cup, black, and went back to my desk. Making the coffee calmed my nerves a little, helping me continue our conversation.

"She supposedly loved me and wanted to be with me. Blah, blah, blah. She thought she could tame me. That's never going to happen. It was when I started having sex with some Demons down here that she became truly evil. I couldn't have that amount of evil down here, so I banished her to purgatory. You never want to go there, never mind for the rest of your life. Especially when you are immortal.

Listening to Tempest tell her story, I couldn't help but think how wrong humans got it all. She said she and her brother created a story. Was that where everything we were taught about Heaven and Hell came from? Did God really write the bible? That was something I had never believed and still found hard to believe. It took me a minute, but I realized she was still speaking while I was lost in my thoughts.

"Now, we've had many people come down and then complain when they ended up here permanently because they didn't follow the rules. They would take their complaint to Hell Court. The judge is one of my daughters, Celia, and she's so resentful that she always lets them go."

I got up and started pacing around my office. I'd told this story more times than I could count, but it was still hard talking about my kids. Over the years, I'd become more chill. I didn't stress over things for too long like I used to. The problem was my kids still remembered the Demon I was as they were growing up.

I never would have won Mother of the Year. My kids all moved to Heaven to be near their uncle and cousin Jesus long ago. Over the past 20 years or so, they had begun coming down to visit me. In fact, we wanted to plan a family reunion.

Celia would say, 'How could they know the rules if you didn't tell them the rules?' Where the Hell was the fun in that? If people knew the rules, they would follow them. Anyway, the ruling government of Hell said we must tell everyone the rules. Why did I ever allow a government to be formed? After all, I am Satan! I rule Hell. Okay, that's funny even to me.

"I will give you the rules of being a human down here in Hell. Once you know them, there is no longer a way for you to challenge that ruling. So, I would suggest following them. Here they are!" She handed me a piece of paper that I glanced at quickly.

Stay at least 500 feet away from my compound. Things that are top secret go on there. Unless I or one of my generals invites you, stay away from my compound. If you get an invitation from anyone else, say no. No other invitation is valid.

You must always wear your ID. That is more for your benefit. Although most of the Demons down here won't hurt anyone, some of them fall for humans. Becoming a Demon's lover is usually how humans end up being told they can't leave. Demons fall way too fast and want to keep the first person who they fall for. Especially when it's a human.

There is only one more rule here in Hell. Have fun! No one ever gets to come back once they leave, so enjoy your time here. Unless you decide to stay here with a Demon or you end up here at death. You'll regret ending up here at death.

"Do you think you'll be able to follow the rules? If not, tell me now. I hate it when we have problems with humans."

Well, the rules of Hell were easy. I was pretty sure I could remember them in my sleep. But what were the chances of Tempest falling head over heels in love with me? I wouldn't mind staying down here if I could be her lover.

What was I thinking? Sure, she was beautiful. The most beautiful woman I'd ever seen. She was also Satan. The actual Satan. And we were in Hell. No woman could be that beautiful. *I must be losing my mind. Or she has me under a glamor.* "Yes, I'm sure I'll be able to follow the rules. They don't sound that difficult."

"It's time for me to go back to my compound. We have a big concert tonight, and I need to be ready in time since I'm the host. You can come to the compound for the concert if you'd like. I'll let the Demon at the door know I have invited you if you decide to come. You can ask anyone you meet where the compound is. Everyone down here knows how to get there. If you come, I'll see you there. If not, I'm sure I'll see you around. Don't forget the rules. I'll have Abaddon, one of my generals, show you to a suite at a hotel downtown. If I don't see you tonight, we'll talk soon so you can interview me for your book."

CHAPTER TWO

abaddon

PREPARING for an event at Satan's compound in Hell was never easy. At least one Demon always ended up in jail in the castle's dungeon. Tempest was even bossier that day. It was as if she was nervous about something. Which was weird. The Devil rarely got nervous. She told the chief guard that an extra guest might join the festivities. There was a rumor floating around that he was a human down there for a book he was writing. The rumors also said that Tempest had a thing for this human. Whoever was spreading these rumors had better be careful. There might have been a cell in the dungeon with their name on it. Tempest was very fair, but she hated rumors about her personal life.

Tempest only required two guards in her quarters, one at her bedroom door and one on her balcony. I wouldn't have wanted to be one of those guards. If someone, somehow, got into the Devil's quarters, both guards would have lost their heads. Whether it was their fault wouldn't have mattered. You might have thought losing one's head was extreme. You would have been right. Luckily, a Demon's body parts grew back, including their heads.

I couldn't help but feel like I was just walking around. Everyone was doing what they should be doing. Which was normal at Satan's compound in Hell. You would think it was because Tempest was a boss who wouldn't tolerate mistakes. After all, she was the Devil. But that wasn't the case at all. Most of the time, Tempest was a fair boss. It took a lot to make her angry unless it affected her safety. Demons lived endless lives, and most of her staff had worked at the compound for hundreds, sometimes thousands, of years. The pay and benefits were great, and like I said, she was a fair boss. People stayed as long as they could.

Suddenly, I felt my phone vibrate in my pocket. As soon as I hit enter, I heard Julian, another guard, talking. "Don, have you seen Tempest? The cook is looking for her. Something about not wanting to cook meat. Why are so many Demons vegetarians? One reason I was looking forward to this is the food. If there is no meat, what's the point?"

As soon as he called me Don, I lost track of everything else he said. I hated that nickname. "Julian, you know better than to call me Don. My name is Abaddon. I haven't seen Tempest. Have you tried her office? I don't have time for this right now. I'm sure you can find her if you tried." Hanging up, I continued walking around the castle, ensuring everything was running as planned.

I was just about to go into the banquet hall when I heard someone call my name. "Abaddon!" I spun around. The beauty before me took my breath away every time I saw her. If only she could see me as more than a guard. Lilac was Lilith's youngest daughter. At only 21, she was already gorgeous.

She had her mother's long blonde hair and bright green eyes. She was 5 feet tall and had curves that could bring most men and Demons to their knees. Me included. But it wasn't her looks that drew me to her. It was her personality. She was so sweet and caring. That was rare in many Demons but even rarer in the daughters of Lilith. She was nothing like her mother or her many sisters.

"Lilac, how many times do I have to tell you to call me Don?"

A pretty shade of red brushed across her cheeks. Maybe she at least knew I was interested. It would make sense since I'd had Demons put into the dungeon for calling me Don before. I found it highly disrespectful to call a top general by a nickname. Lilac was a different story. I would love for her to be less formal and call me Don. No one would call me ugly. At six foot four, I was tall, even for a Demon. My blonde hair fell just past my shoulders, usually unintentionally messy. My blue eyes were the color of the deep blue of oceans on Earth, and my muscles had muscles. I had both female and male Demons hitting on me all the time.

All except for Lilac.

Not only had Lilac not hit on me, but she had also ignored all my attempts to hit on her. She either disregarded them or didn't see them for what they were. Lilac was rather naïve, which was odd for an inhabitant of Hell. That was just another reason that I found her so enchanting. Could it be that I wanted what I couldn't have? No, I didn't think that was it. There was just something about Lilac that made me want her forever. I had often wondered if she could be my true mate. Even though I had watched thousands of Demons find their true mates, I had never been sure I had one, never mind one of Lilith's daughters.

Knowing Lilith, I hadn't believed Lilac was worried about what her mother thought. Lilith had zero motherly instincts and didn't care what her daughters were doing. Being one of Tempest's main personal guards would have made me highly attractive as a son-in-law in Lilith's eyes, even though I was hundreds of years older than Lilac. Whatever it was, I was going to break through her walls.

Wait, was she talking?

"My mom asked me to look for you. She wanted you to make sure the gardens had some of Tempest's top generals tonight. She heard a rumor that soldiers from the other side would try to come in through that area."

"Can you let your mother know that we also heard that rumor? We'd added excellent security in the gardens. If anyone tries to come through there, they'll be in a cell in the dungeon before the night is half over. Now, onto happier topics. Do you have a date for the concert?" I had to take my shot. I had been waiting too long for her to show some interest. It was time to stop hinting that I was interested and ask her out.

She slowly lifted her face to meet my gaze. She looked at me shyly, her eyes partially hidden beneath her long eyelashes. "I don't have a date for the concert. I thought about not going because it's such a big night in Hell, and I didn't want to go alone."

That would not do. If I wanted anyone at the concert that night, it was Lilac.

"Well, we can't have that. The castle not having your beauty would have been a great travesty. Would you do me the honor of being my date tonight?" I held my breath while waiting for her to answer. Being one of Tempest's top generals, I was rarely nervous. Yet, I found myself nervous while I waited for her answer.

"I'd be happy to be your date, Don, but won't you be guarding Satan?" Well, at least she was finally calling me Don, and she had said yes to the date. Had it always been that simple? Was asking her on a date all I needed to do? It certainly looked that way.

Luckily, Tempest had given me the night off to enjoy the concert. Nothing was stopping Lilac and me from going together. I looked into her eyes and grabbed hold of her hands. Electricity immediately ran through me as soon as we touched.

"Tempest gave me the evening off. She knew I'd been wanting to see this group in concert for years, and I wouldn't be able to enjoy it if I had to watch out for her. Can I pick you up at 7:00? The dinner before the concert begins promptly at 7:30, and Tempest would not appreciate it if one of her top generals was even one minute late. I know you don't live too far away, but I suspect there will be a lot of traffic."

She looked surprised, which made sense. Tempest giving me

such a big night in Hell off had surprised me, as well. But she was a fair boss.

"That sounds great. I'll be ready."

I wanted to high-five someone, but whom could I high-five? Plus, I wasn't sure Lilac would appreciate it.

CHAPTER THREE
just another day in hell

I AWAKENED this morning from a dream about myself and Jacob. It was hot as Hell. The things he was doing to my body in that dream. I enjoyed it so much that I almost had the Demon who woke me up sent down to the dungeons for a year or ten. My legs still trembled from that dream. If just dreaming about him could bring out such intense feelings, what would it be like to be in his arms for real?

I finally gave up staying in bed and trying to continue my dream when Blade continued banging on the door to my quarters for at least five minutes. I got out of bed and grabbed my robe, sulking.

Yes, Satan sulks.

By the time I got to my living room, the banging had calmed down a little. Perhaps the Demon on the other side of that door could sense my annoyance. Blade was an empath, which was rare in a Demon. I walked over to the door, grabbed the doorknob, and yanked open the door.

"Blade, this had better be good. I told you and Samael I wanted to sleep in this morning and for no one to disturb me until I woke up. What is so important that you would defy a direct order?"

Blade kneeled on one knee and hung his head. He had the good sense to look sheepish. I knew it was only an act. Blade wasn't afraid of me at all. However, he respected me, and I suspected that was what this act was all about.

"Blade, get up. We grew up together, and you fell from Heaven shortly after me. You know there is no need to kneel before me."

"Yes, my Liege, whatever you ask. I am at your command." Now he was just being a jerk. This man was one of my best friends growing up. "Now you're just being impossible." I walked away from the door to sit on my white leather couch. "Don't just stand at the door. We're not having a conversation over there. Come, sit down."

Once we were both seated, it was time to ask again why he would disturb me when I asked him and Samael, his brother and the second man who guards my quarters, not to do so. While Blade's post was outside my door, Samael's was on my balcony. "Now, what is so important that you had to wake me up?"

"There's been a human at the door three times this morning. He said his name is Jacob, and you permitted him to come to the compound." I felt my face heat and could have smacked myself. Blade would catch that. "That's a delightful shade of red there, Tempest. Is it crimson?" he asked, chuckling. "Don't tell me you're going to take another human as a concubine. The human doesn't look like your type at all. He doesn't look like a nerd."

He's got jokes this morning. "Forget what I said about us being childhood friends. You can go back to treating me like your liege now." I was only kidding, of course. I knew many people thought a man and a woman couldn't be friends. However, Blade and I had been friends since before kindergarten. I wanted my friend, not a subject.

"Now we both know that will not happen, Satan. Unless, of course, I want to bust your balls." He really was a smart ass.

"Since when do I have balls, Blade?" I looked at him with the most innocent look I could muster. I knew he meant metaphorically, but that didn't mean I wouldn't give him a hard time.

"Tempest, you can try to look demure, but I know the real you. So, you want to tell me about this Jacob person? He's not bad looking. If you're not interested..."

I loved Blade, but he was a Demon whore. Few men stood a chance when he decided he wanted them. He could be charming when he wanted to be. I'd never seen his allure; however, he had left a string of broken hearts scattered around Hell.

Blade was a nice guy and enjoyed being in love. However, he wasn't looking for his one true mate or any type of long-term relationship. My friend was more of a love-'em-and-leave-'em type. Everyone in Hell knew it, as well as many people on Earth with knowledge of Demons. No one paid attention. They all thought they'd be the ones to change him. Men could be as bad as women in thinking they could change someone.

"You go near him, and I will have you beheaded." This time, I was almost serious. What was it about Jacob that made me crazy? I squirmed in my seat. One thing I never wanted was to appear like I had an Achilles heel, even in front of my closest friends. There wasn't much I hid from my friends. That was one of those things.

Blade just laughed. "This reminds me of when you met that Angel about a hundred years ago and thought he was your one true mate. You told him, and he was so scared because, well, you're Satan. You threatened to behead me when I invited him down here to have dinner with you. That was the last time you threatened to behead me." He laughed as he said that until he saw the blush that crept across my face again.

"Tempest, no. Do you think your one true mate might be a human? That would make me so happy, my friend. You deserve to find love. I know you try to maintain your reputation as a badass. You may be Satan, but I know you better than that. You've also proven it often with the way you mete out punishment. As often as you threaten the worst punishments imaginable, you never actually do it. You are almost as kind as your brother."

"Do not compare me to God, Blade. You know I can't stand him." Of course, that wasn't true. Did my brother and I have a complicated relationship? Absolutely. Our history was fraught with problems, stemming back to before I jumped out of the Pearly Gates. We've had problems since we were children.

"I know no such thing, Tempest. You and God both pretend that you hate each other, but everyone around all those many years ago knows that you both miss the relationship you once had. You don't think we discuss it when we all get together?"

I smiled sadly at him. He wasn't wrong. I missed my relationship with my brother. He was the best big brother a girl could have asked for. I just didn't know if we'd ever be able to repair our broken relationship. "Tell me again why my brother and I don't forbid the angels and Demons from mingling?"

His green eyes bored into mine. "Because neither of you is cruel. You both know that those of us who began in Heaven miss our families that are still there. Neither of you would ever demand that we never see our families again." Again, he wasn't wrong.

"Can I ask you a favor, my friend?"

I was almost afraid to ask what that favor was. As strong of a Demon as he was, Blade was also crazily sentimental. He was a born romantic, even though he was a Demon whore. Sighing, I responded. "Yes, Blade, you can ask me a favor." I knew what he was going to say. He was going to tell me that if I thought Jacob was my one true mate, I should go with it and let whatever was going to happen happen. Although I wasn't sure I wanted to hear it, I let him finish.

"Don't let the whole 'the devil needs to be tough' crap hold you back from finding love. You've been doing that for far too long. Looking at your face whenever I mention Jacob makes me believe he is your true mate. Don't throw that away."

I needed to change this conversation now. "You know, you look like your dad when you're all serious." His dad stayed in Heaven with the woman he met after his mom came down to Hell. His dad also drove him crazy. He was constantly trying to get Blade to return to Heaven, and Blade was having none of it.

When we all originally jumped, my brother and I had a lot of anger toward each other and Demons and angels had to stay on their own turf. As we slowly began to heal our relationship, we realized that wasn't fair to either side. Many Demons still had family up in Heaven who they missed and who missed them. My brother and I decided the best thing to do would be to allow travel between the two planes. But Blade hated returning to Heaven, even for just a short visit.

Blade started laughing. "You didn't just go there. I never looked like my dad. He may be handsome in his way, but I'm way better looking. You are your brother's twin when you're serious. Even more so when you're angry."

I grabbed the throw pillow behind me and threw it at his head. Hard. It wasn't like I hadn't heard that before; I had. Many times. Blade knew better than anyone how much it irritated me.

"Now you're pushing it, Newman." He caught the pillow before it could hit him in the face. My aim was spectacular, but he was faster than most Demons, and that was saying a lot. As much as I was enjoying this, it was time for us both to get to work.

"I need to get dressed and get some work done before the festivities tonight. You and Samael are relieved of your duties for now. Grab him and get out of my quarters. If Jacob comes back, tell him I'm busy working, but I look forward to seeing him tonight."

He bowed. "Yes, my Liege."

I grabbed the pillow, laughing. I responded in my 'Satan' voice, "Get your brother and get out!" It didn't scare him at all. He laughed as he walked over to the balcony door to get his brother before leaving my quarters. Samael waved to me as they were leaving.

Hopefully, I would forget about Jacob long enough to get some work done. I ran Hell like a well-oiled machine, and from the outside looking in, it looked easy. Only it wasn't. Hell was a big place, with mostly Demons living there. Demons might not be as bad as most people thought, but they still liked to act up occasionally.

Demons tended to think they were so different from Angels. We weren't that different, though. It was almost like different countries on earth. There were differences between the countries, but the people were similar. Even my brother would admit that Demons weren't the enemy. After we all jumped, there was a lot of anger on both sides, and we lived with that anger in different ways.

Angels acted, well, angelic after we jumped. Some Demons acted out, even though it was their decision. It took years for us to realize that we were angry. We had left what had been our home for more years than most of us remembered. Most of our families stayed up there, and we missed them. We had jobs we left. There was so much loss. With so much anger, it was easy for violent crimes to run rampant, and they did.

Those early years were when my reputation began. If I hadn't taken control, Hell wouldn't have survived. None of us would have survived. Many Demons tried to overthrow me because they liked the way Hell was. They thrived on the chaos that was Hell during the early days.

Those early days were also where the human idea of Hell and Demons came from. We were every inch what humans thought, from our looks to our actions. When we fell, something happened to each of us. Our skin became dark red, and we had a tail, hooves, and horns. The day I realized we had magic and could use a glamor to change our appearance would always be one of my favorite days.

Changing our appearance didn't change the way we acted, though. It took my brother and I mending our relationship for me to realize I wanted more from my people. Realizing Hell would never be a perfect society, I still wanted to make it better.

It was then that I began to form Hell's elite guards, with original Demons training some of the Demons born in Hell to be fighters. Not just fighters; a lot of them were already fighters. The original

Demons taught them the discipline they had learned during their many years in Heaven.

Hell and Demons didn't transform overnight. Some Demons never truly changed; they simply stopped the violent crimes. Most of them. The ones who kept up that behavior met a violent end. Some were in between, not completely evil, but not good, either. They spent years in the dungeon in the castle until we were sure they could contribute to society.

did blade go too far?

HAVING SPENT most of the day working, I was finally almost finished ready preparing for tonight's festivities. As I was putting on my shoes, there was a knock on my door. Since almost everyone at the castle was still getting ready or already downstairs in the ballroom, either working or mingling, I couldn't help but wonder who it could be. Since it wasn't time to leave, I saved my feet for a little longer by waiting to put my shoes on. The purple stilettos matched my dress perfectly but still killed my feet.

The person knocking on the door became more insistent. "I'm coming, I'm coming." Everyone was so impatient today. By the time I got to the door, I heard someone whistling. That someone sounded suspiciously like Blade. "You again? Can't the devil even get dressed without being disturbed? The Demons start rumors if I'm not looking my best, you know that. Now, what can I do for you?"

"Well, you can start by changing the purple paint covering this living room. I mean purple. Really? A nice glossy black would look great with your white furniture." Was he serious? My decorating skills were not up for debate. Ever.

"I wasn't talking about my decorating skills, Demon!"

"Yes, you did. You mentioned Demons start rumors about you. Most of the rumors are about what drives your decorating of Hell. The guesses range from you being color blind to you being batshit crazy. Me? I go with the theory that you're batshit crazy." Sometimes, I wondered if I needed this friendship with Blade. Other times, I cherished my relationship with my oldest friend.

Besides, he was right. Some Demons weren't quiet when insulting my decorating skills. I didn't see the issue. Hell had a lot of color; I liked it that way. Okay, so it had a lot of pink and white. They were colors. When we were creating Hell, it was very dark. A lot of black and gray. It matched the attitude of a lot of us at that time.

Once we started changing, I found myself wanting Hell to be filled with brightness. Since Hell was so far below the sun, its light didn't reach us. That meant it was always dark. I began by adding artificial lighting so it would appear that the sun came into Hell. That was one change most Demons were happy with. What they didn't like was when I began adding pink all over Hell.

"Okay, you think I'm batshit crazy? What else is new? Now tell me what you want." Looking at him, I noticed he had a smirk on his face. "I won't like this, will I?"

He chuckled before responding. "Jacob came by again." This would not be good. He looked so happy about Jacob coming back. I gestured for him to continue. "I might have told him you told me you want him to be your date to the party and concert tonight." I bit my tongue so hard I tasted blood before responding; it took me a minute to realize he was still speaking. "I also may have told him you would like it if he got here early so you could have some alone time before dinner." That did it. Even my closest friends should know better than to push it that far.

I somehow spoke while grinding my teeth. "You. Did. What?" I slowly rose from the couch, but Blade did not back down. He continued to justify his actions as if I wasn't his boss.

"Don't act all Satan-like with me. You know it won't work. You're into him. I could see that from a mile away. After speaking with him for ten minutes, I could tell he was also into you. Does this mean he is your one true mate? I can't answer that. But I will not sit around and watch you throw another one away. You're one of my closest friends, Tempest. I want to see you happy. I'm not saying you're unhappy, but you deserve more. You deserve love."

It was time I told Blade about my genuine fear. "He's human, Blade. What if he is my one true mate? I love Hell, I think it's great. But what if he doesn't? If he's my one true mate and we start something, how could I survive if he went back to Earth? Not all humans feel the one true mate pull like supernaturals do. What if he is my true mate, and he feels the one true mate pull? Will my subjects accept him running Hell by my side? I'm not sure I can allow him to become a Demon just because of me."

While being a Demon wasn't that bad, it wasn't for everyone. For instance, I was sure that Jacob had a family. Would they be able to accept Jacob if he became a Demon? How about if he moved to Hell? Sure, he could visit them; they could even visit him here. It wouldn't be the same, though.

Then there was our true form. While most Demons used a glamor, some didn't because it took a lot of work to use that much magic on a regular basis. We all let the glamor go at night once we were home. Which brought up another issue. How would Jacob feel about seeing me in my true form?

Being Satan's one true mate would also hold a lot of responsibility and be a lot of work. If he decided to become a Demon, my people would expect him to run Hell by my side. If he decided to stay human, that would not be an issue. He couldn't run Hell with me without being a Demon. His title would be Prince Consort.

There would be so much to consider if Jacob and I were to be together. But that would be for another day. Tonight was for the Demons of Hell to come together and enjoy each other's company.

"Tempest, I know you think the Demons here in Hell don't like our lives, that we all accept our lives but don't like being Demons. You know better than most how many of us jumped from Heaven, and you know we still can go back to Heaven if we choose and at least try to resume our lives as angels. How many Demons have done that? And how many of us have stayed down here in Hell? We're happy, Tempest, and if Jacob is your one true mate, he would be happy too. I know you would make sure it was his decision. If he decides he wants to remain human, he'll still be able to stay in Hell with you. He just won't be able to take the throne beside you. Is having someone rule by your side more important than living your life with your one true mate?"

Every word he said was true. In my heart, I knew that. My heart wasn't the problem, though; my head was. I was overthinking this. I didn't even know if we'd like each other, never mind if he was my one true mate. "You're right, Blade. I'll spend time with him and get to know him. If there is nothing there, we have lost nothing. If we are true mates, we have a lot to gain. I guess I have a date tonight."

I couldn't help the smile that came across my face. "Ummm..." Now I was nervous again. "He may or may not be knocking on your door any minute." As soon as the words were out of his mouth, someone banged on my door.

"Blade!! Demons can't even just come up to my quarters and knock on my door! Never mind a human who has been here less than 24 hours! What were you thinking?

"You know as well as I do, he's not just some human, Tempest. I would almost bet my entire collection of Armani suits he is your one true mate. I'm not asking you to invite him to move to Hell and the castle. I'm simply asking you to get to know him." Blade had wanted the best for me since we were children. I doubted that had suddenly changed.

"I know you haven't spent much time with him yet. And I've only met him a couple of times. But I see the look on your face when you talk about him. You light up. I've never seen that look on your face before, and we've known each other for a really long time. Although he may not feel the mating pull, he is feeling something. He blushes when he talks about you. Actually blushes. A grown-ass man. He's feeling something, too, Tempest. It may be nothing. However, you owe it to yourself to see what happens."

He was right. There was something between Jacob and me, even though we hadn't spent more than a half hour together. It didn't make sense to me other than, like most supernaturals, Demons recognized their one true mate as soon as they met.

"Okay, let me answer the door, then you get out of here. I don't need one of my oldest friends as a chaperone." Not only didn't I need one of my oldest friends as a chaperone, but I also didn't need a chaperone at all. I'm older than dirt and have been on millions of dates.

"Speaking of your oldest friends, do you think he'll mind being involved with a cougar? After all, you are a few years older than him... A few thousand years older than him." Sometimes, I had to remind myself that I loved this Demon and would miss him if he wasn't here. But if I sent him to the dungeons, I could visit him.

"My beauty and sexual prowess will convince him that being with a cougar isn't so bad. Now come on." He gagged as he got up to join me. Just the reaction I wanted. I knew thinking about my sex life would get rid of him.

"Ew, I don't want to think about your sexual prowess. That's just gross, Satan." Yeah, locking him in the dungeons was looking better and better. I slowly walked to my door when Blade grabbed my hand and pulled me along. When we arrived, he didn't even wait for me to open the door. He grabbed the handle before I had a chance to. "Hey, Jacob. Welcome to Satan's lair," Blade said as soon as he saw Jacob standing there.

I rarely used my Hellfire; however, I still knew how to use it. I zapped Blade on his ass before pushing him out the door.

I heard him yell before he took off to do whatever he was going to do. "Tempest! You know that stings! There was no need to zap me." His footsteps were heavy as he stalked away from my quarters.

"Come on in, Jacob." My hands were clammy, and I could barely walk straight because I was so nervous. I made my way over to my couch and expected him to take the chair next to me. Instead, he sat beside me on the couch. Almost afraid to make eye contact, I looked down at my hands. It was only a moment before I felt his hand on my chin, gently raising my face to look at him.

"Tempest, is it okay that I'm here? Blade made it sound like you wanted to see me, but if not, I can leave and see you at the party tonight."

He was such a gentleman. If he is my one true mate, did I deserve him? That was a question for another time. I shyly shook my head no. "While I didn't know what Blade was doing, I'm glad he talked to you." That was an understatement. Having Jacob in my quarters felt right.

"When information about the paranormal community came out on Earth, it was all such a shock. I never thought I would meet anyone who was not human, yet here I am, talking to Satan herself. Who, until yesterday, I believed was a male. I have a lot to learn. Honestly, I don't know what to think right now. That's not completely true. I don't know exactly what's going on, but I know that I'm drawn to you in a way that is new to me."

His words made me happier than I ever thought possible, and I couldn't stop myself from grabbing his collar and pulling him in for a kiss. Damn, he could kiss! As soon as my lips met his, I couldn't stop the moan that escaped my lips. *It's only a kiss, Tempest. Breathe. If he asked to move into the castle right now, I would probably say yes. It feels like we're made for each other. Oh!*

We finally pulled apart after about ten minutes of tonsil hockey. Ten minutes that felt like 60 seconds. "Jacob, I don't know exactly what's going on either, although I have an idea. I'm hoping you'll stay long enough to figure it out." I looked down again, nervous about what he was going to say.

He walked me over to the leather couch in my living room, sat down, and pulled me onto his lap. "I want to find out more than you can imagine, Tempest." My dark heart beat double time at his words. Something told me this man could be the end of me, but I didn't care. I wanted him more than I wanted my next breath.

CHAPTER FIVE

a human is my one true mate

TEMPEST GROANED as she looked at me. "What's the matter, beauty?"

She huffed and sat back on the couch. "I wish we could stay in my quarters all night getting to know each other. I could have called down to the kitchen and had dinner sent up to us. We could have spent the night talking, which would have been fine. I just want to get to know you better. We have about an hour before we need to leave for the state dinner. It doesn't help that it's going to be an extremely long night. I know you're staying at our best hotel, but would you like to stay here tonight? Again, we can talk all night. No pressure. I just hate to be away from you now that we've spent a little more time together."

The peculiar thing was that I felt the same way as her. This truthfully made no sense. That wasn't the point, though. I needed to figure out what was going on, which would mean spending more time with this gorgeous woman. That won't be a hardship. "I don't understand what's going on, Tempest, but the thought of leaving your side causes me pain. Actual physical pain. I'm not sure I could leave you if I wanted to, and truth be told, I don't want to."

She smiled at me ruefully. "I know what's going on, Jacob. I promise we'll discuss it when we get back here tonight. There's just not enough time for that conversation right now." They said curiosity killed the cat. Well, I was glad I wasn't a cat right now. I got up and started pacing across the living room. "Tempest, it's okay. We don't have to discuss it right now. I have a feeling that no matter what it is, it won't change anything I'm feeling right now."

"How about we take a walk around the castle? Maybe I can introduce you to some of my top Demons. Frankly, I'm having a hard time being alone here with you without ripping your clothes off." That sounded like a good plan to me, but we needed to be someplace in an hour. So, clothes had to stay on.

"I'm all for that, but I have a feeling tonight is important to you. So put your shoes on, and let's get out of here."

She looked at me with a cocky smile on her face. God, I already love that smile. "I think maybe we both should freshen up. You have a little lipstick on you, and I'm sure my lipstick needs to be fixed."

I couldn't help but snicker at that. She looked beautiful, but her lipstick was a mess, and I didn't want to walk around with lipstick on me.

It took us a little longer than we planned to freshen up. We were having a hard time keeping our hands off each other. If I wasn't sure before, I was now. Jacob was my one true mate. You would think being Satan would make it easy to tell him this. After all, Satan didn't get scared, did she? Well, yes. Yes, she did.

Admittedly, it took a lot, but I got scared. Most of my fear stemmed from interpersonal relationships. I'd never been good at them, and I usually screwed them up. Finding my one true mate who was a human? Scary as Hell! How was I going to explain all of this to him? Luckily, supernaturals came out to humans years ago, so they understood things like the one true mate theory. But how would he feel knowing he was Satan's one true mate? That was a lot different from knowing about the one true mate theory.

By the time we stopped kissing and were both freshened up, we had just under a half hour before we had to be at the banquet hall for dinner. "I would like to do a quick walk around the banquet hall and the ballroom. The President of the United States is supposed to arrive in about an hour, and I want to make sure that everything is just right. Are you ready for a date with the devil?"

He smirked at me. "You think you frighten me, Satan? I've had dates with women who were so much scarier."

Although I laughed at that, I wasn't happy to hear about the other women he dated. This mating pull was a bitch. My body felt like it was on fire, and I was having a hard time keeping my hands to myself and focusing on what we were talking about. All I could think about was being with him. It was similar to the feel of a new relationship, only 1,000 times worse. I was sure he was right, though. I'd met some women on Earth. Their crazy could out crazy my crazy sometimes.

"Then tonight should be a piece of cake for you." Until we got back here, and I explained that he was my one true mate. This could break me if he didn't take it well. But for now, I'm going to enjoy our evening together. I took his hand. "Come on, Jacob. Let's go explore the devil's lair."

He grabbed me around the waist and kissed me before tugging us both to the door. Once we were in the hall, the sounds from the main floor floated up to us.

When we reached the last stair, I noticed Abaddon talking to Lilac, Lilith's youngest daughter. That was interesting. Abaddon has been asking Lilac out since she turned 21, about six months ago. He had been interested in her since she turned 18, but he wanted her to turn 21 before he pursued her. She had been ignoring all his attempts. Until now, evidently. I whispered in Jacob's ear so he could hear me above the noise. "Come over here. I'd like to introduce you to one of my top personal guards." Abaddon looked up, surprised, as he saw us walking towards them.

"Abaddon, Lilac, it's so nice to see you both here. Lilac, have you been able to visit your mother lately?" Lilac looked at me with her eyes shining. There was something between her and Abaddon, but she didn't see it. Abaddon knew she was his true mate, but she couldn't see it. She should have recognized it as soon as she turned 18.

"Yes, I went to Purgatory and spent the week with her last month. Thank you for allowing her to have trips to Hell. Like most Demons, I hate Purgatory. Since both of my parents are there, I spend more time there than I would like to." I understood how she felt. I spend as little time as possible in Purgatory.

Purgatory wasn't necessarily a bad place. There just wasn't a lot to do there other than work. Everyone in Purgatory had a place in keeping it running smoothly. The sun was the exact opposite of Hell, too. The sun shined very brightly in Purgatory, which made it extremely hot. Demons were sent to Purgatory when their crimes were numerous, and the dungeon in Hell would not hold them.

This applied to Lilith because, being an original Demon, her magic was strong. Keeping her in the dungeon would have been difficult. As much as she hated Puragoty, she would have hated that more. At least by being sent to Purgatory, she had somewhat of a life. The only way to leave Purgatory was through a special portal in the center, which required a bracelet to be given to Demons when they visited the place. She was also able to spend time with Bill, her last husband, and Lilac's father.

Bill was a good Demon until Lilith finally gave in to his advances. There was something about Lilith that caused men and women alike to lose their damn minds. Like Lilith, Bill's crimes began small, such as petty theft. It wasn't long before Lilith and Bill were Hell's very own Bonnie and Clyde.

Their crimes were numerous, and I let them go as long as I could. That was one of the worst ideas I'd ever had. Their final crime was robbing the largest bank in Hell. Not only robbing the bank, but also killing several guards who tried to stop them.

After a long trial for each of them, it was decided they would be sent to Purgatory. The sentencing was not easy, in large part because of Lilac. She was so young at the time, but even though her parents would be taken away from her, she could still visit. If we decided on the death penalty, Lilac would have never seen her parents again.

"Your mom has been doing much better, so I expect we'll grant her next appeal to come back to. Don't tell her that, though. I don't want her to get too confident. It would be interesting to see if she could continue to control her behavior if she returned to Hell."

"That's great news, Tempest. I agree. Letting my mother know such news before it happens would benefit no one, least of all her. Hopefully, my dad will return sooner rather than later, so I can stop visiting Purgatory."

"Once your mom is here, she'll be able to petition for your dad to be allowed back if she wants to, and I don't see why we would deny that petition. Your dad has been staying there to be near her." Lilac beamed at that. She was and always would be a daddy's girl.

"I'm so sorry. I'm being rude. This is my date, Jacob. This is Abaddon and Lilac." The three of them shook hands, and Abaddon looked at me curiously. I had a feeling that Jacob and I had been a topic of conversation around the castle. "Abaddon, what's that look all about? Wait, let me guess. That a human has been coming around today, asking for me, has caused rumors to float around the castle."

Abaddon looked at me sheepishly, and Lilac hid a smile behind her hand.

"You don't have to answer. I can tell I'm right by the look on your face. Rumors about the devil are nothing new, Jacob. I hope you can get used to it." Abaddon reacted to what I said immediately.

"You hope he can get used to it? What's going on, Tempest?"

I had to laugh at his reaction. Even though I was the devil, some of the oldest Demons were very protective of me. We'd been friends since childhood, and they all acted like my older brothers. Especially since God was up in Heaven. They thought I needed older brothers down here, too.

"Can I discuss it with Jacob before I discuss it with you, Don?" Now, all three of them looked at me with shocked expressions. Oh God, why me?

"Of course you can, Tempest. I have to ask if you think having a human here tonight is a good idea. The rumors of the opposition attacking the castle tonight are still floating around. If the rumors are true, it will be dangerous enough for Demons, never mind a human."

While he did have a point, if we didn't allow humans in Hell because of rumors about the opposition planning an attack, humans would never be allowed in Hell. "I understand your concerns, Abaddon, but I have faith that the Demons protecting the castle will also be able to protect Jacob. It's not like he'll be the only human here. Remember, the President of the United States and the First Gentleman will also be here. So everyone is already prepared for anything that could happen."

I could see the concern in his eyes, but he also knew it was my decision. He had already tried to stop me from having the President attend the event; however, I refused to rescind the invitation since it had been planned for about a month. My guards were well prepared to handle whatever happened tonight. At least, I hoped so.

CHAPTER SIX
all hell breaks loose

WE HAD BEEN at the dinner for almost an hour when the U.S. President arrived. Demons throughout the room were getting antsy because we held dinner until she and the First Gentleman arrived. It was never good to make Demons wait for food. Our metabolism was excellent, which often meant we were desperate to eat at mealtime.

Luckily, I had heard the President was often late. When it was decided that she would be attending, I sent a postcard to every address in Hell, letting people know they should eat something beforehand. As we sat there waiting, I realized that many Demons did not take my advice.

Once standing, I took Jacob's hand in mine, letting him know I wanted him to come with me. He looked at me quizzically, but took my hand. It took only a few seconds before we were standing in front of President Greene. She looked perfectly at home, even though it was her first time in Hell. If I didn't know better, I never would have guessed she had never been in a roomful of Demons before.

"Madame President, it's nice to finally meet you," I said, extending my hand to her. She had a strong handshake and smiled at me. As soon as our hands touched, I felt the magic within her. That was interesting. President Greene wasn't human. Usually, I could tell what kind of supernatural someone was, but I couldn't this time. Why was she hiding it? Humans had known about the supernatural world for years, and for the most part, they didn't care. Hell, most humans would have a bigger problem with a female President than a supernatural one.

"Madame President, it seems you've been keeping a secret. I just can't tell exactly what that secret is." Jacob looked at me with a question in his eyes. I shook my head slightly, hoping no one noticed. It was then that I realized I hadn't introduced them. "Madame President, Mr. Greene, I'd like to introduce you to my date, Jacob. Would you like to join us at our table? I had you both sitting at another table, but I feel we have much to discuss."

"That's a great idea, Tempest. Lead the way." This was turning out more interesting than I thought it would be. Once we were seated, the waiters came out to serve everyone, and the Demons stopped murmuring as they finally began to eat.

The four of us ate dinner. Once we were done, I began to question the president. "President Greene, I couldn't help but feel your magic when we shook hands, but I couldn't detect what kind of supernatural you are."

Jacob's head jerked toward me like I just said the earth was flat.

"Please, call me Monique. I'm surprised you could tell I have any magic. A very powerful witch on my staff mutes my magic. As much as humans appear to be okay with the supernatural community, many still secretly hunt down supes. We have a special FBI department that seeks out these individuals. However, their numbers are always growing."

Although I didn't spend much time on Earth, that didn't surprise me. Some humans were nastier than some of the Demons in Hell. Jacob and I spent hours talking to Monique and her husband, Jack. It seemed that Monique was fae. Before they left to return to the White House, she promised they would invite us to an upcoming state dinner.

It truly had been an idyllic evening. It sounded weird—an idyllic evening in Hell, but it could not have gone better. After that night, I hoped the President of the United States would realize that Hell was not an awful place. Did we have some issues? Of course. But so did Earth. We were no worse than them, but it was taking a while for people to understand that. After our conversation, I suspected President Greene would not have any doubts about that.

Sometimes, I wished supernaturals had never come out from hiding. I didn't have to reveal myself when they did. However, they all knew about me, my brother, Hell, and Heaven. While my brother didn't let just anyone visit Heaven, Hell was open to anyone. Lots of people, human and supernatural alike, loved my brother, but he didn't trust many. He had a strict vetting process before anyone could visit Heaven. He had major trust issues with the angels, never mind others. So many supernaturals had been down here over the years, and we had no vetting process. As long as people let us know they were coming, they were welcome.

Keeping the secret would have been next to impossible. So, God and I got together and discussed what we should do. It was the first time he and I had been in the same room in about a decade. Deciding was easy since it turned out that we were on the same page about letting people know we existed, as did Heaven and Hell.

Of course, people loved hearing about God. He held multiple press conferences for adoring audiences. Unfortunately, people weren't so happy to hear about me. Most of them believed all the stories about my brother and me and, of course, I'm the bad guy, umm, girl. That was the main thing that surprised them. Satan is a beautiful woman instead of a red-skinned man with horns, hooves for feet, and claws.

My brother also surprised them. God was six feet tall with long red hair, the same shade as mine, and green eyes. God looked very similar to what people on Earth thought Jesus looked like. He might have been my brother, but I could admit he was handsome. He also didn't have a halo.

As for my nephew Jesus, let's just say he was nothing like people thought he was. I loved my nephew, and we had a great relationship. He came down to Hell often. He was also one of the few reasons I went up to Heaven occasionally. But again, that's a story for another time.

I thought it would be great for Jacob and me to go out to the garden. It was a beautiful night, and the garden was gorgeous. It was one of my favorite places to relax, sit, and think when I had a lot on my mind. Few people knew because it was one secret we kept to ourselves that the garden outside the back of the castle walls was the Garden of Eden. Yes, that Garden of Eden. We kept it a secret from many people, including the Demons down here. Only those who had been here since the beginning knew the truth. We did that because our enemies would destroy it if they knew what it was and the power that it held.

God had always wanted the garden to remain in Heaven. As much as I loved it, I couldn't blame him. It was moved because a faction of Angels who wanted to destroy my brother somehow discovered that humanity would cease to exist if the Garden of Eden was destroyed. Adam and Eve were its original inhabitants, and all humans were descendants of Adam and Eve.

Adam and Eve should have never died. They were true immortals like my brother and I. No one knows exactly how it happened— although there is a theory that Eve wanted to leave the Garden, and Adam was heartbroken. So before she could leave, he killed her and then took his own life. Once they died, their essence was absorbed into the soil and flora of the garden. If their essence were to be destroyed, it would be as if they never existed. That would make all humankind cease to exist.

After the faction of Angels tried to destroy it, my brother called me up to a meeting of the highest council of Heaven. Against my brother's wishes, they had decided the garden needed to be moved to Hell because no one would expect it to be there.

"How about we go out to the garden? I'd love to show it to you. It's beautiful this time of year. Plus, it is a gorgeous night out."

Jacob placed my arm in his and started steering us towards the garden. He had never been to the castle before, but a wall of windows overlooked the garden, so it was hard to miss it.

A deck led to the garden, and the door to the deck was open. I took a deep breath when we got outside, breathing in the fragrant night air. "Wow, I've never seen a garden this beautiful, Tempest. You must have magnificent gardeners." If he only knew what made the garden so beautiful.

He wasn't wrong, though. The garden was beautiful. Almost every type of flower there was filled the garden. Roses that couldn't exist anywhere else in Hell due to the composition of the soil thrived in this garden. In the center stood a large marble statue of Aphrodite. On one side of the garden was a waterfall with stairs leading down to the only hot springs in Hell. I'd spent many hours relaxing in the hot springs.

I looked over at him slyly, wondering if I should tell him the truth. Maybe tonight when we had our other conversation. "It is beautiful, isn't it? I come and sit out here, on that bench over there, when I need to relax or if I have a lot on my mind. It is the perfect place to think about things."

We were walking over to the bench that I pointed to when a bunch of my guards came running into the garden, their guns drawn. I immediately thought of the rumors about my enemies being here tonight and entering the castle through the gardens. I grabbed Jacob's arm and pulled him back into the castle. Normally, I would have wanted to be in this fight. However, I didn't want Jacob to get hurt. He was my top priority.

I watched out the windows as my guards pulled several men and women out from deep within the garden. I might not have been involved in it right now, but I could keep an eye out in case they needed me. My guards seemed to have it all under control, but when I saw one man Abaddon had a hold of, I couldn't help but gasp. Abaddon caught my gaze and looked like he might have tears in his eyes. It wouldn't surprise me. It was Gusion, one of Abaddon's closest friends since childhood. Gusion was one of the original Angels who fell from Heaven. My heart broke for Abaddon and me.

What I couldn't figure out was why Gusion was involved in this. The leader of the opposition wanted to take my place. While we didn't know who it was, we'd had Demons defect from his side who told us he treated them horribly. Unfortunately, the Demon had a very powerful witch in his pocket. We figured that out when we realized the Demons who defected couldn't tell us anything about him or his plans other than he wanted to unseat me. They were physically unable to say anything. They would start choking whenever they tried.

Being one of the original Demons, Gusion had it very good under my regime. Don't get me wrong, as long as Demons acted appropriately, they all had it good under my regime. But the originals were my top guards, and they lived a very good life. Every original that wanted to had a suite in the castle, and they were each paid very well. That's why it was a mystery why he would turn against me. There was no doubt that life in Hell would change dramatically if this Demon took over. While we had no way of knowing exactly what changes he would make, we did have intel that told us he would be a dictator and the freedom that Demons now enjoyed would no longer exist.

I asked Jacob to stay in the grand hallway, but he refused. I had to trust that between myself and my guards, he would remain safe. During the dinner and concert, Abaddon had a conversation with the guards and let them know they were to protect Jacob as they protected me. From the way Abaddon looked at me when we talked earlier, I could tell that he guessed Jacob was my one true mate. That meant that he was to be protected as they protected me. Because in Hell, that was what being a leader's one true mate meant.

When we got to the door, Jacob stopped me. "Are you okay, beauty? You look like you've seen a ghost and might be ready to cry." It felt good that he cared so much. I would explain to him later who Gusion was, but now I needed to get outside.

"Satan doesn't cry." I smiled at him, but even I could hear the tears in my voice. "Seriously, I'll be okay. But right now, I need to be there for Abaddon. As upset as I am right now, he must be heartbroken. That man he's holding onto with his left hand is one of his childhood friends. He jumped shortly after Abaddon did. Which wasn't long after I jumped out of the Pearly Gates."

"I'm coming with you." I smiled at him, and we walked over to my friend and guard. As we walked over, Abaddon handed the two Demons he was holding onto to another guard. The look in his eyes told me finding this out crushed him. None of us could have seen this coming.

"Hey, how are you doing? I know this can't be easy. Truth be told, it isn't easy for me either, knowing that one of my oldest friends has turned against me. But I'm more worried about you right now." Being closer to him, I can see that his eyes are glassy. As suspected, he is on the verge of crying—not a simple thing for any Demon to do, especially for an original Demon and one of my guards. Crying is something that our counterparts in Heaven did, not us.

"I'm not okay, not by a long shot. But I will be. I can't believe that Gusion turned against you. You're a fair and just leader. That asshole who is leading the other side is neither fair nor just. He kills his people at the drop of a hat, not even asking for explanations. All that is needed for one of them to be beheaded is for him to hear a rumor. Why would Gusion do this?"

"I know I rarely allow guards to interrogate criminals here in Hell. However, if you'd like to go down to the dungeon and question him, you have my permission. This is hard for me because you know what my punishments usually are like, no matter what the crime is. It's going to be hard to mete out my usual form of justice when I think he deserves so much more."

"Tempest, that's who you are. You have a good heart, no matter what humans think. I know this is hard, and he deserves so much more. But you need to be true to yourself. Can I give a suggestion?"

I smiled at my friend. "Yes, you may." I couldn't wait to hear this.

"I think you should turn him into a tiny, white, fluffy cat. One that some socialites would want to carry in a purse. Then, I would love for him to be sent topside to be a witch's familiar. Preferably a terrible witch or a young one just learning her powers."

I heard Jacob snicker beside me. "Is that the type of punishment that Satan metes out?" Then he started laughing hard. Looking at it from his point of view, it was funny. But I wouldn't say that to him.

"It is a punishment that I would give, yes. Now stop laughing." He tried unsuccessfully to pull himself together. "I'll take that under consideration, Don." He gave me a quick hug before rushing off to question Gusion. He was going to hate this punishment. I grabbed Jacob's hand in mine. "Let's go to my quarters. It's been a long night, and we need to have a conversation."

CHAPTER SEVEN

having the conversation

WHEN WE GOT up to my quarters, I didn't know what to do or how to begin. But I thought sitting down so we could relax would be a good place to begin. After kicking off my shoes, I finally looked back at Jacob. "Hey, why don't we get comfortable so we can talk? The couch is quite comfy. I've been told my decorating skills suck, but I choose furniture well."

Jacob chuckled. "I was wondering who picked the paint for the walls. It's a lovely shade of purple."

"Move it, human. Before I go all devil on you."

He chuckled again and went over to sit on the couch.

One thing I knew for sure was that I couldn't sit too close to him. We'd be in each other's arms in no time, and we would never talk. While I hoped the night would end that way, I didn't want it to happen until he knew what he was getting into with me.

The look on his face said he noticed I was not sitting near him, and he looked disappointed. "I'm only sitting over here for now while we talk. I promise I hope this night ends with us much closer." That seemed to cheer him up, although he still looked lonely sitting over there.

Since he does not know what's going on, I should be the one to begin. It took me a minute or two to find the strength to do so. "I'll be honest, in all my many years, I've never had to have this conversation. The more I think of it, the more I realize that's a good thing." He looked like he was going to say something, but if I didn't get this out now, I might never.

"I want to hear what you have to say, but just give me a minute to get this out." He shook his head, his eyes full of questions. Hopefully, he would like the answers. "This may be the first time I'm grateful that my brother and I came out when the supernaturals did. This way, I don't have to explain as much to you."

I took a deep breath to gather my thoughts a little before continuing. Jacob sat there patiently, waiting for me to continue. Okay, I can do this. I'm the devil, after all. "Jacob, how much do you know about the one true mate theory?" His eyes bulged, but he didn't look completely surprised.

"I know all supernaturals have one true mate, or at least that's the leading theory. Judging by the way I feel when I'm around you and how I feel physical pain at the thought of being away from you, you also have one true mate. And that man is me."

He wasn't running for the door. Maybe that was a good sign. "Yes, Jacob, you're right. Honestly, after all these years, I didn't think I had a true mate. It's not that I haven't been involved with both men and women. After all, I am extremely old. It's that I've never felt the true mate pull for any of them. Some of them have been extremely powerful, I mean Lilith. But not one of them was any more than a sexual partner." He looked a little hurt at that. "Jacob..."

"No, wait, Tempest. I know what you're going to say. We didn't even know each other. Hell, for many of the years you've been around, I wasn't even born yet. Mentally, I understand that. I know how insane it is for me to be hurt that you've been with other people. But it is what it is. Don't get me wrong, I will not let it come between us. I don't think I could if I wanted to. I just want you to know it exists."

"I wish I could say I don't understand, but I do. The thought of you being with anyone other than me makes me see red. Believe me, the devil seeing red is not something positive. While I don't know exactly how old you are, I know you must be at least in your thirties. Which means you've had people in your past. As much as I know that makes sense logically, I also want to find every one of them and scratch their eyes out."

He chuckled. "I get it. So much so that I want to go to purgatory and show Lilith what I think about your history with her. Since you know her and I don't, do you think I could take her?" Now that was funny. Lilith almost has the strength that I do. Almost.

"Baby, I never want to lie to you. Lilith could tear you apart without breaking a nail."

"Okay, we'll forget that idea. Where do we go from here, Tempest? Is there any way that we can be together? Will the people of Hell accept me as your one true mate? I have to say I'm praying that the answer to both questions is yes. I'm not sure I could handle it if they're not."

"You'll be happy to hear that the answer to both questions is yes. There are a couple of ways we can be together and, as for my people, they'll accept you with no problem. No matter what those on Earth think of Hell, my people love me. I treat them right and make sure that they all have what they need. And if they can't provide for themselves, I provide for them. People are content here, and at the risk of sounding conceited, I know they love me. Well, most of them. You saw with your own eyes tonight that some people don't. That's because others want to take my place, though. In any political system, some people want to become rulers. Most places have elections. We don't. That's one thing about Hell that's different. I've always been the leader, and unless someone can take me down, I'll always be the leader."

"Take a breath, Tempest. I have a feeling you're nervous, but I don't want you to be. If we can be together, we'll make it work. Whatever we must do, we'll do it. This brings me to my next question. What do we have to do to be together?" So far, this had been easy. The rest should be a piece of cake. There was no reason for me to be nervous.

"There are a couple of ways that we can be together. What you must remember is there is one thing that has to happen in ways before we can be together. You need to move to Hell. Permanently. Honestly, the only way we'll both be able to be happy is for you to move into the castle. I wasn't sure in the beginning if you would even feel the mate pull since you're human. But since you do, you won't be happy anywhere other than by my side. Same for me."

I held my breath while I waited to hear his answer. "Tempest, I plan on moving here as soon as possible, but I always want to be honest with you. As much as I feel a pull toward you, this is not an easy decision. I'll be leaving my family and everything I've ever known. Explaining it to my parents will be even harder."

I could finally breathe. That was the hard part. He had a choice on whether he became a Demon. We could be together either way, and my people would love him either way. I wasn't foolish enough to think all would be smooth sailing. That's not the case for any couple, even true mates.

"Since you're okay with moving to Hell, we can be together easily. There's a choice to be made, which is completely in your hands. Just remember that we'll be able to be together whatever you decide. So don't feel that you must make one decision over the other. I'll be perfectly happy either way."

He looked nervous again. Was I not explaining this right?

"What is this choice that I need to make? You make it sound like a big decision. Although I am glad that whatever it is, I can choose for myself."

"You're right. It is a big choice. It's also one that I don't want you to make right now. I'd prefer that you think about it first, maybe talk to a few other Demons. One choice will change nothing; the other will change a lot. The choice is if you want to become a Demon. I rarely offer to turn humans. Most humans don't even realize that I have that power. We already have a lot of Demons down here, and more arrive every day. That's why I don't just go around turning humans, or supernaturals, into Demons.

It was time to tell him how to turn someone into a Demon. While it wasn't a horrible process, it wasn't fun, either. That was why some people turned it down. Not many, especially if they were given the opportunity, because they were mated to a Demon. But some still declined.

"Jacob, before you make a final decision, I want to describe the process to you." I took a deep breath before continuing. "Remember when I hit Blade with hellfire earlier? He nodded his head yes but didn't look too nervous... yet. Probably because when I hit Blade with hellfire, it was a little zap.

"While the process does involve hellfire, it's not a simple zap like I gave to Blade. All Demons have hellfire running through our veins; it's a part of who we are, so it's not something we even feel. However, unless you're born a Demon or end up in Hell after death, I have to transfer hellfire from me to you. While it is an easy process, it's also very painful. Hellfire is exactly what the name implies. It's fire from the depths of Hell. I would touch you and essentially push it into you. Since I have unlimited hellfire in my body, I'm able to give whatever is needed."

I paused to give him time to take in what I had said up until that point. Once I thought he was ready to hear more, I finished. "We would sit back in recliners side by side, and while I was touching you, the hellfire would transfer to you. Not every touch causes this; it has to be my intent to infuse a person with hellfire. It takes a long time, usually between two and three hours. It will feel like it is burning you from the inside out as it enters your body. Once it is done, you will be a full Demon."

He tried to look like it didn't scare him, but I could see the fear in his eyes. "That's all? To be honest, I figured I would have to turn into a Demon. Knowing I have a choice makes me feel better. I agree with you. Since the choice is mine, it's not one that I'm going to make

SATAN, IS THAT YOU?

tonight. I may not even make it soon, but I will decide if I want to remain human or become a Demon. I like your idea of talking to Demons about it. I'm going to do that."

At that point, I did what I'd wanted to do since we left my quarters earlier. I pulled him to me and kissed him as I'd kissed no one before. This conversation was the hard part. We could talk about everything else later.

CHAPTER EIGHT

the morning after

WE WOKE up at about 10:00 am, which was late for me. I'd usually have been in multiple meetings by now. Since Jacob and I still had some talking to do to figure out exactly what we were doing, I texted Blade and Samael late last night to let them both know not to disturb me. I briefly explained the situation, but they already suspected Jacob was my mate, so they understood.

When I woke up, Jacob was still sleeping, so I called down to the kitchen to have a nice breakfast sent up to us. I was just getting out of the shower when I heard Blade letting the waiter into my living room. Once I heard the two leave my quarters, Blade flirting with the waiter the whole time they were there, it was time to wake Jacob.

I walked over to him and pressed a kiss on his forehead. I could think of better ways to wake him, but after last night, we both needed a little sustenance. His eyes fluttered open. "Well, good morning, beauty. How long have you been awake?" He looked so good with his hair tousled.

"Long enough to have breakfast brought up. Ready to get up? I waited for Blade and the waiter to leave to wake you up, but it won't stay hot for long."

I saw a twinkle in his eyes and knew he was up to no good. "You're the devil. Can't you just blow on it or something to heat it?" he joked.

"Oh, you think you're funny, do you? No, I can't just blow on the food and heat it, although that wouldn't be a rotten trick. I'm always eating in my office while working, and a lot of food ends up cold." He looked at me like he didn't appreciate that comment much.

"Tempest, if I'm going to move down to Hell, I don't expect you to spend all your time in your office. Don't get me wrong, I know you have to work, and I'll be looking for a job, too. But we also need to make time for each other." He wasn't wrong, and I had no intention of spending more time in my office than needed. He didn't have to work, either, but that was something I'd never say to him. Some men didn't want a woman to take care of them.

"I have no intention of spending any more time in my office than I need to, Jacob. So, there is no need to worry about that. We will also have dinner together every night, so make sure the job that you get will allow that. I know this may sound strange since I always have people around me, but I was lonely before last night, Jacob. People were around me constantly, but it was never enough. I never realized it, but I needed you. I've had other people in my life, but even when I was seeing someone, I was lonely. No one was ever enough. Now get your ass out of bed so we can have our now-cold breakfast. I don't make the staff deliver meals more than once." I grabbed the sheet and pulled it off him as I spoke.

"Bossy. I like it. It's kind of hot."

I looked at the lopsided smile on his face and couldn't help but giggle. Yes, Satan giggled occasionally. I had a feeling it would become a regular part of my life now. I melted onto his lap for a good morning kiss.

"I'll show you bossy, baby. I'll even buy a whip if you'd like. We sell a lot of those down here." He looked at me with that grin again, and my heart did flip-flops.

"You mean Satan doesn't own a whip already? Shouldn't that be part of the punishment when people are bad in Hell?" Now that was funny. For all the stories about how horrible I was, whipping someone would never be a punishment down here in Hell.

"You remember the punishment that Abaddon and I discussed last night, right? The one where I may turn Gusion into a fluffy kitten and send him to Earth to be a witch's familiar?" The look on his face told me he was holding back a laugh.

"How could I forget that? I still don't believe that Satan turns criminals into white cats to be witches' familiars as punishment. What does your brother do, send people on vacation as a punishment?" I had to snicker at that. Humans took the rumors about my brother and me to heart.

"Trust me, Jacob, you don't want to hear about some of my brother's punishments. Yes, he might have some punishments as I do, but God's punishments are sometimes much worse than mine. Believe it or not, our jobs are very similar. We have some great Demons down here in Hell, and my brother has some Angels up in Heaven that aren't very heavenly."

The more that Tempest and I talked, the more I realized that nothing I knew about Heaven and Hell was true. Or at least very little of it. Since I'd be living in Hell, I had plenty of time to learn about both places. I guessed I'd be meeting God and Jesus as well. It sounded like Tempest was close to her nephew, and while she might not be close to her brother, she loved him. I'd seen a little of Hell, and I couldn't wait to visit Heaven.

"Okay, why don't I throw some clothes on, and we can have our cold breakfast?" I stole a quick kiss before getting up. Where did I leave my clothes last night? I'd go to the hotel later to get my things. Since this was supposed to be a quick visit to Hell to interview Satan, I didn't bring much with me.

"I asked Blade to have a bathrobe delivered. It's in the bathroom in the hallway. I didn't want them to disturb us by bringing it in here. Do you think you can run to get it naked without someone coming in?" Satan thought she was funny. She just wanted to see my ass as I ran for the closet.

CHAPTER NINE

preparing to go topside

JACOB and I held tight onto each other's hands as we walked down the stairs to the main hallway. It was hard for us to stop touching each other, and I couldn't help but wonder if it would always be like this. "Jacob, I was thinking we could go sit in the garden to talk some more. I want to tell you a secret about the garden, too."

By the time I finished speaking, we were at the bottom of the stairs. Jacob started walking towards the garden, never letting go of my hand. "A secret about the garden, huh? Let me guess, it's the Garden of Eden, and somehow it ended up here in Hell."

I stopped short, my mouth agape. Jacob looked at me like I had just grown horns. I knew he couldn't see my horns because I kept my glamor on whenever around anyone. "No, it can't be. I was joking," he said, surprised. I walked again, pulling him along behind me.

This was not a conversation I wanted to have in the great hall of my castle. Too many people could be around that weren't close enough for us to see, and the great hall was like an echo chamber. I couldn't allow anyone to know the garden we were heading to was THE Garden of Eden.

I could hear him stuttering behind me as he tried to catch up. "No, it can't be. How would that be possible?"

By the time we got out to the garden, Jacob had calmed down a bit. He also caught up to me. I no longer had to pull him along. Instead, I could guide him over to the bench I wanted to sit on last night. I put my finger over my mouth to ask him to be quiet. He sat there looking at me, no longer saying anything. "Yes, this is the original Garden of Eden," I said as softly as I could so he could still hear me.

"Why are you talking so softly? And why is that my question when I just found out I'm sitting in THE Garden of Eden?"

I shushed him again before I continued. "I'm talking softly because even here in Hell, very few people know the truth. We don't know how everyone would react if they knew. We hope everyone will revere the garden as those of us who know the truth do. As it should be. However, we know there would be people who'd want to destroy it. Just like some people want to destroy my brother and me, some people want to destroy everything that still exists from the beginning. My brother and I don't know who everyone is that wants to do this, but we know there are some in both Heaven and Hell. While we have caught some of them, we know there are more. Sadly, we'll never know if we have them all."

It still hurt more than I could explain that Gusion was involved in this. I'd been trying not to think about it, but it was hard. He and Abaddon were closer than he and I, but all of us originals were still very tight. When we jumped, it was just us. We had nothing but each other, not even a place to live. It took a lot to build Hell, but we did it together. No matter how hard I tried, I couldn't figure out why he would turn against us.

"Wow, I don't even know what to say or to think, if I'm honest. This is incredible. I don't even know where to begin with everything that you just said. Wait, I know where to begin. No wonder your garden is so beautiful. It's the Garden of Eden. Thank you for sharing that with me. Please know I would never break your confidence."

"I know you wouldn't. If I didn't, I never would have told you this, nor would you be moving in with me. Speaking of which, we need to make plans to go topside so you can clear things up and get your things." He looks surprised again. I'm getting to know that look.

"You're going to come with me?" he asked. He sounded like he thought I wouldn't. Did he not want me to? Maybe he was ashamed of me?

"I was hoping to, if that's okay." I hoped it was okay. Introducing Satan to your family as your one true mate when you were a human wouldn't be easy, but I would love to meet his family, even if we didn't tell them who I was.

"Of course, it's okay with me. I just wasn't sure you'd have the time or would even want to. I can't wait to introduce you to my family. I know it's going to be a lot to take in, but once they get to know you, I'm sure they'll love you the way I do. And if not, can't you smite them or something? Maybe turn my little brother into a pet? He's annoying."

I slapped him on his arm. "I'm not turning anyone into a pet. As far as me having time, I have great people who work with me to get everything done. They'll be fine handling everything while we're gone. How about you go get your stuff from the hotel and bring it back here? I'll pack for our trip topside?"

"Wait, what? Do you want to get ready to leave today? Are you sure you'll be able to leave this quickly? I can be ready as soon as needed, but it doesn't have to be today."

"It won't take me long to be ready at all. One phone call to Abaddon to let him know he's in charge is all it will take to cover work. He's my right hand when I'm not here. Blade and Samael will be happy to have some time off, especially Blade. He and the waiter who delivered our breakfast this morning seemed to get along well. I have a feeling they'll take advantage of the opportunity to spend time together. I think when I call Abaddon, I'll make sure he gives the waiter the time off work, too. Blade will appreciate that."

"Satan will give a waiter off so he can have a tryst with one of her

52

top guards?" He was trying not to smile, but I could see the corners of his lips raising ever so slightly.

"Yes, I would. But it isn't completely selfless. I know it will make Blade happy. Keeping the guards, especially my guards, happy benefits me, too. But to be honest, it is mostly for Blade. I saw them interacting during dinner last night, and I could see he was very interested. I enjoy seeing my friends happy, so sue me."

He grabbed me by my waist and kissed me soundly. "I think that's one of the sweetest things I've ever heard. My family is going to love you!"

Suddenly, I was feeling nervous. "I hope so. I'd hate it if they didn't." He looked down at me, putting my hair behind my ear.

"Beauty, I know they're going to love you, but even if they don't, it won't change things between us. I'm in this for the long haul. Since you're Satan and I'm probably going to be a Demon one day, the long haul is a very long time." He wasn't wrong.

"Why don't you head to the hotel? I'll be ready to leave when you return. We'll have a quick lunch, then head out. A portal in the garden will take us wherever we want to go on Earth."

We kissed again, and I walked him to the main door. Before we came down, I called to have a driver wait outside to take him to the hotel. Once he headed out, I went up to my quarters, feeling lonely already.

CHAPTER TEN

meeting the parents

IF JACOB DIDN'T GET HERE SOON, there was going to be a hole in my living room rug from my pacing. I got past my nervousness after Jacob assured me his family would love me. However, I was not known for my patience. I wasn't sure what was taking him so long to get back here. I'd been ready for about 15 minutes already. Granted, I only had to walk up to my quarters, and he had to travel halfway across Hell and back, but come on. I was ready to head topside.

Finally, someone knocked at my door. Why didn't I give him a set of keys? He wouldn't feel like this was his home if he had to knock on the door when he needed to come in. I grabbed the extra keys sitting in a bowl on the side table beside the door.

I opened the door and handed the set of keys to Jacob as soon as I opened the door. "Whoa! What are these? That's a lot of keys to get into our home."

I giggled. I enjoyed it when he said 'our home.' "You're right. It's a lot of keys to get into our home. It's the keys to most of Hell—not every key to the doors of Hell, but the keys to everything I need access to. We'll go over what door each key goes to later. For now, this is the one that will let you in here." I pulled the gold key out to show him.

"A gold key to open our door? Isn't that a lot?" He chuckled. I couldn't argue with that.

"Yeah, it is a lot. It wasn't my idea. I had left the key making to Abaddon. He thought he was funny. I figure it at least made it easy to find the right key when I came home drunk." I shrugged.

"Where are your bags? Weren't you getting your things from the hotel?"

"Yeah, I left them downstairs, in the great hall. I figured since we were going right back out, I didn't need to bring them up here. The guard at the door put them in a closet for me. Are you bringing all those bags with us? How long do you plan on being on Earth? A year?" I packed a lot, but I always did. I never knew if I'd need something.

My black card worked on Earth, but I enjoyed having my things. It made me more comfortable, which was needed because Earth made me itch. I wasn't allergic or anything. It just wasn't my favorite place to be. "I am bringing them all. Blade said he would come up to help bring them down because he knows how much I pack. I just called him through our telepathic connection, and he's on his way up."

It wasn't that Earth was a bad place; it wasn't. About 50 years ago, I had a bad experience there that never left me. Work had been overwhelming me at the time. Everyone wanted some of my time, and I had none for myself. That's when I decided an extended trip to Earth was in order. Although humans knew about Satan in a general sense, no one knew it was me. I could be Tempest while on Earth, not the leader of Hell.

Up until that time, I had always enjoyed spending time on Earth. In fact, once my brother and I began to fix our relationship, we would take a trip together every couple of years. This time, I met a human. He was the exact opposite of Jacob in looks and attitude. Jet black hair, lanky, and moody as Hell. I still thought he had been my one true mate until I met Jacob. That was why I wasn't positive Jacob was my mate the minute I laid eyes on him. I thought my one true mate had come and gone.

Being Satan was not something I could keep from my one true mate, especially since I had to live in Hell. I'd never forgotten that conversation. He didn't believe me at first. When I first told him, he laughed, thinking I had to be joking. When I didn't laugh back, his face paled, and that's when I knew he believed me. It got ugly, and fast.

I wasn't sure how I hadn't seen the darkness in him. The stupid man thought he could take down Satan. Since I still had feelings for him, I couldn't kill him. Instead, I used my magic to take away any memories of me, leaving the memories of before that time intact. That was when my punishments changed and became something most people wouldn't believe if they heard them.

It took no time for us to get down to the portal in the garden, with Jacob and Blade carrying my bags. I could carry my bags, but it felt nice to have people take care of me for once. "How are we going to get all of this through the portal? It's a lot."

"The portal is much bigger than it looks once inside. I have a car with a Demon driver waiting for us on the other side, and he'll help us with our bags." I carried our bags into the portal when I noticed Jacob wasn't moving.

"You know just where the portal needs to take us?" Okay, that's just weird. His one true mate was Satan, and he found it weird that I would know where we were going. Out of everything that had happened the last two days, that's what he found strange?

"Are you serious, Jacob? I'm Satan. Finding out where we needed to go was easy. I can't believe that out of everything that you've learned in the past two days, you find that weird. Is it any wonder I love you?" As soon as that was out of my mouth, I wanted to take it back. Not that I didn't love Jacob, I did—with all my heart. I just didn't know how he was going to take it. We both knew what being true mates meant, but did it mean he loved me already, too? This was

56

not a conversation I wanted to have as we left to meet his family. He didn't look shocked at all, though.

"Why do you look so scared, Tempest? You should know that I love you with every fiber of my being. I do not doubt that you love me, so saying it shouldn't scare you. Hearing the words come out of your mouth makes me thrilled. So, just in case I wasn't clear enough, I love you, Tempest. More than I could have ever imagined loving anyone. We can stay here and discuss how much we love each other, but I believe my parents are waiting for us at their house."

He had the most adorable smirk on his face. "No need to discuss it as long as we're both on the same page. Let's go meet your parents! That's one sentence I've never said in my life and never expected to say."

While Jacob did travel to Hell in a portal, he never traveled in one of my portals. Being Satan had some advantages, and one of those was super-fast portals. When we arrived at the other side, he looked a little green around the gills.

"What the Hell was that? I feel like the trip pulled my body apart, molecule by molecule, and then put it back together. Why would you travel that way?"

I couldn't help but laugh. "You'll get used to it, baby. It's an experience that is difficult the first couple of times. But by your third time traveling in one of my portals, you'll feel as if you have always traveled that way."

"The third time? Can't we have his and hers portals? You travel in yours, and I'll travel in mine? I think that would work better for me."

"You'll be fine, baby. Now, let's grab some of our bags, and the driver will grab the rest. Let's get to your parents' house. I can't wait to meet the people who brought you into the world. I'll never be able to thank them enough." Jacob and I started grabbing our bags while the driver picked up the rest. On the way to the car, the driver let us know that there was very little traffic, so we would arrive at my future in-law's house in no time.

Great, no time to prepare myself. I thought I had prepared myself while I waited for Jacob back at the castle. However, the knots in my stomach told a different story. Once in the car, Jacob grabbed both my hands and held onto them. I had a feeling that was not only because he could sense that I was nervous but also because he was anxious.

When we pulled up in front of the house, I saw an older couple on the porch waiting for us. Shoot! I never asked Jacob if he explained the situation to his parents. Before I had the chance to ask, our driver was at my door and opening it. He held his hand out to help me out as if I were a princess instead of Satan. That always made me laugh, and this time was no exception. It also helped me to relax a little.

Jacob walked over to my side of the car and took my hand as our driver took our bags to the porch. As we walked to the porch, the ripples in my stomach turned into a full-on tsunami.

When we got to the top of the porch, I expected his parents to shake my hand or something. What I didn't expect was for his mom to pull me in for a hug. After all, her son had just brought Satan home to meet them. Jacob had called his parents and had a talk with them about me. They knew he had been going to Hell to interview Satan, so they hadn't been completely in the dark. When she finally let me go, she started talking right away. "Tempest, it's so great to meet you. I must be honest; I never expected Satan would one day be visiting our home, never mind be our son's mate."

Jacob explained everything to his parents. What did he say his mom's name was again? Oh yeah, June. And his dad was James. "It's very nice to meet you, June. I will not lie. I never expected to even meet my one true mate, let alone that he would be human. So, it seems we're both experiencing the unexpected."

I grabbed James' hand to shake it when he also pulled me in for a hug. While he did that, June hugged her son. "Tempest, it's so great to meet you. It's about time our son met the one for him. We've been waiting for him to move out for years. I know kids are staying home longer these days, but 38 is a bit much."

The look on his face told me he was giving his son a hard time. They both looked at Jacob like they loved him more than life itself. Being his parents, they probably did. God and I don't haven't had parents for more years than I can remember, so it's always hard for me to understand what it's like. But I understood a little more when I saw how the three looked at each other. I also couldn't help but hope that Jacob and I would have children one day. "It's great to meet you also, James. Your house is lovely." God, I was so bad at small talk with humans.

"Thank you. Why don't we go inside, and you can see the rest of it?" He grabbed a couple of our bags, but Jacob stopped him and looked back at our driver. Our driver shook his head and began picking up the bags. Jacob handled the rest.

"We have the bags. Why don't you show us where you'd like us to put them?" The men went inside while June came over and put her arm around my waist. "It is great to have you here, Tempest. We've waited so long for Jacob to find the right woman, and here you are! We're so happy for you both."

She had tears in her eyes, which made it even clearer how much she loved her son. "It's great to be here, June. I love your son more than I can say, and it is such a pleasure to meet you and James. Why don't we head on in, and we can get to know each other better?"

CHAPTER ELEVEN

while the devil away, will the demons play?

WHEN TEMPEST first called me to let me know I would be in charge while she and Jacob went topside to meet his parents, it annoyed me. Although Hell ran relatively smoothly, it still took up a lot of time. Luckily, Tempest knew that Lilac and I had just begun dating because she said that I could work strictly eight-hour days if I made sure that I was on call 24/7. That wasn't a terrible deal at all. I would have to work eight hours a day if I was in charge, and being on call wasn't bad in Hell. There was rarely anything to do.

That was why, when I woke up this morning, I called Lilac and asked her to go out to dinner with me tonight. She agreed right away. Part of me was nervous that she would say no, but the other part was confident she would say yes. We had a great night at the concert and dinner, and we both clarified that we wanted to see each other again when I brought her home. I asked Lilac to pick the restaurant as I wanted to do something she wanted.

We had some excellent upscale restaurants in Hell, so I thought wherever she chose would be great. Lilac was like her mother in one respect. She preferred the finer things in life. That was why I was sure we wouldn't go to one of Hell's burger joints. Lilac did not disappoint me. She told me she would think about it and call me back when she decided where she wanted to go. It didn't shock me when she told me she chose the best Italian restaurant in town. I was almost expecting it.

Although there wasn't much happening in Hell, I couldn't wait to finish my day. Things were so slow that I spent most of the day in my office working on payroll for the castle staff. I hated doing payroll, but if I didn't, no one in the castle would get paid. That included me. Not that I needed the money; I was banking most of it to buy a house in Hell. I already own one topside on Cape Cod. It wasn't that I didn't enjoy living in the castle; it was just that it was time I finally got my place. If I was honest with myself, I knew I should have moved long ago.

I considered traffic when I left to pick up Lilac. I told her I would pick her up at 6:30, and that was when most Demons were getting out of work. So, the traffic was heavy. With the time I gave myself, I should get there just in time. As long as I wasn't late, I'd be happy. If I was early, I could always wait in the parking lot across the street from her house until 6:30. It was always when I was in a hurry that Demons tried to test my patience—almost as if they hadn't heard about my reputation. Most of the time, I was very laid back. Not tonight.

I was just pulling onto Lilac's Street, with ten minutes to go, when a Demon decided it was a good time to drag race. He must have been smoking something, and I don't mean bud. I flipped him off and kept going on my merry way. When he saw me flip him off, he looked at me and saw whom he was messing with. He waved, smiled, and drove down the street at a slower speed. I didn't care that he was speeding. That wasn't even a crime in Hell. I just didn't want anyone to disrupt my night with Lilac.

By the time I got to Lilac's house, I was only two minutes early, so I parked in her driveway and went to get her. She must have seen me because I saw her come out her door and lock it. God, she looked gorgeous. Her long blonde hair was pulled up into a high ponytail with wispy tendrils loose framing her gorgeous face.

Her magnificent curves were on full display in a tight black dress so short that if we were on Earth, it may have been illegal. I knew it would have been illegal in Heaven. Heaven was very strict when it came to what people could wear. Skirts had to be no more than a half inch above the knees, and no one could wear pants that were too tight. Bikinis were strictly forbidden. Women could only wear one-piece suits. Luckily, they didn't have to be covered from head to toe. God had tried that, but he was overruled by the high council of Heaven. Lilac also wore black high heels that showed her legs off perfectly. I wiped my chin in case I was drooling.

Shoot! What was I thinking? I hastily got out so I could walk her to my car. Once in front of her, I gave her a quick kiss and grabbed her hand. "You look beautiful tonight, Lilac."

She smiled shyly. "You don't look so bad yourself, Abaddon."

I shook my head, pretending to look sad. "When will you call me Don? I thought we had gotten past the 'Abaddon' stage when I dropped you off the other night."

She giggled and blushed that deep crimson that looked so beautiful on her. "I guess we did, Don."

We walked slowly to my car. I didn't know about her, but I wanted to enjoy every minute of tonight. No rushing in anything that we did.

Traffic had slowed down earlier than usual tonight, so we got to the restaurant about fifteen minutes before our reservation. I expected to have to wait for our table, and I would have enjoyed sitting at the bar and having a drink with Lilac while we waited. The restaurant was extremely busy, so I thought that shouldn't be a problem. Until I saw a maître de coming towards us with menus. No one made original Demons wait in Hell.

Although I sometimes enjoyed the perks of being one of the first who fell, I mostly didn't want them. I didn't want to be treated as if I were special just because I was amongst those who created Hell with Tempest and the other original Demons. Sometimes, like now, I hated it. Sitting at the bar and having a drink with Lilac while we waited for our table would have given us more time together.

But I would not let that bother me. It was what it was, and I couldn't change it. They were not moving someone from their table to give it to us; they just made sure our table was ready early. I would have been happier if they were moving someone away from their table early. That would have given me a reason to say, 'No, it's okay, we'll have a drink at the bar.' Lilac and I were still holding hands as we walked to our table. We hadn't stopped unless we had to since I took her hand at her house. It was like neither of us wanted to let go of the other.

Once we were sitting at the table, I couldn't pull my gaze from her. I could get lost in her beautiful green eyes. She was the first to speak, which was good because I had been rendered speechless. "Are you having fun being the head Demon in charge of Hell? Have you had anyone beheaded yet?" Now, that was funny.

"I know you're not that old, but you've been around long enough to know Tempest isn't the beheading type. Not to mention all your history classes. Nah, no beheading. If I did that, Tempest would behead me." The thought of that made me chuckle. I'm not sure why the thought of Tempest beheading me sounded funny to me. It wouldn't kill me if she beheaded me, but it would be painful, and I certainly wouldn't be going on any dates for a while.

"Well, we can't have Tempest beheading you. You're beginning to grow on me." Lilac picked up her drink and concentrated on drinking. Judging by the crimson covering her face, what she said embarrassed her. I gently took her glass from her and lifted her chin to look into her eyes.

"While you turn a delicious shade of red when you blush, you don't have to be embarrassed by anything you say to me. You've been growing on me since you turned 18, and I'm happy you're catching up."

She looked at me like she was seeing me for the first time. "You were my very first crush. My mother hated it. It's no secret how she feels about Tempest and the rest of the originals. It's like she forgets that she's an original, too. She blames you all for her being sent to Purgatory, even though her actions caused it and the one who decided it was Tempest, no one else. One time, when I was 16, she tried to make me promise never to be with you. I laughed in her face. You know how 16-year-old girls can be. Even if I was a human, I probably would have laughed in her face."

I couldn't believe what she had just said. I also couldn't understand why she rebuffed my advances for so long. "I've been trying to let you know how I feel since shortly after you turned 18. Why have you always ignored me? You never even showed that you knew I was trying to get to know you better."

It was her turn to chuckle. "For two reasons. One, because I wanted to make you work for it. I didn't want to just give in to you. But more importantly, I wanted to make sure that I was ready. I also didn't feel the mating pull, so I thought it might just be a crush, and one day, one of us would find our true mate, and the other would be hurt. I realized I wanted to take a chance the morning before the event, so you asked me out again at the perfect time."

"Wait, you didn't feel the mate pull? That makes no sense. You should have felt it the day you turned 18. You know what? Let's think about that later. Tonight, I want to enjoy my first date with my one true mate." While I knew there was something wrong with this situation, what I wanted to do at that moment was enjoy the evening with Lilac now that she realized who I was to her.

CHAPTER TWELVE

gusion wants to meet with abaddon

I HAD BEEN DOING WELL at keeping to my eight hours a day, but honestly, it was because of Lilac. Until she finally dated me, I was a workaholic. That was the main reason my bank account was where it was. Not only did Tempest pay all her staff well, but being one of her top generals, my salary was better than a lot of the staff. Tempest also made it a point to give bonuses often for good work. If things kept progressing the way they had been with Lilac, the bonuses for overtime might slow down.

After I had been in my office for about an hour, I got a call from one of the dungeon guards. It wasn't a big surprise, but I wasn't looking forward to it either. "Ruby, what's up? I'm working hard running Hell over here. Can it wait until tomorrow?" I heard the redhead's throaty laugh. I knew she would know I was trying to avoid the inevitable.

Ruby was also one of the original Demons, and she was hurting almost as much as I was over Gusion's betrayal. I tried to talk her into allowing one of the newer guards to watch over Gusion during her shift, but it was a no-go. She probably felt it was her duty since he was one of us. Ruby was the only original Demon guard who worked in the dungeon, and she seemed to feel that one of us should be there while he was there. She asked Tempest if she could change to 16-hour shifts while he was in the dungeon. Tempest said no.

We all knew that even an eight-hour shift was a lot for one of us, but Ruby wouldn't budge on at least working her regular shift—even after Tempest told her she could have a paid vacation for as long as Gusion was down there. Ruby refused, and when Tempest tried to push the issue by pulling the "I'm Satan" card, Ruby said if Tempest forced the issue, she would go on an extended vacation to Earth. We all understood where she was coming from. I was one original who asked to be stationed in the dungeon for as long as Gusion was there. Tempest said no to that as well.

"Abby, I take it you know what I want?" I growled into the phone. She knew I hated it when she called me Abby, but she did it often. Too often. She got a kick out of my reaction.

"Ruby, it's Don or Abaddon, you know that. You know I hate it when you call me Abby." Ruby just laughed again. Some days, I almost forgot she was one of my oldest friends and retaliated. Almost.

"Don, you know I do it to give you a hard time. You're so easy sometimes. Anyway, I'm sure you've been waiting for this call. Gusion wants to meet with you. He not only wants to meet with you, but he also wants to do it outside of the dungeons. Tempest had a feeling he would want that, so before she went topside, she let me know when it came up that she approved it. He didn't say where he wanted to meet with you, but you have permission to pick him up and go wherever he wants to talk. You have as much time as you need."

Why did Tempest do this? What was she thinking? I wasn't worried about being able to handle Gusion alone. Not only was I more powerful than he was, but I also knew that he would never hurt me. I also knew, without a doubt, where he wanted to go. Tempest knew, too. I thought that was why she said yes. "Can you give me about an hour, Ruby? I need to make a phone call and finish some work here, then I'll go down to the dungeon and pick up Gusion."

"Of course, I can wait. What else do we have to do down here? Gusion hasn't been going anywhere for a while except with you, and I have another four hours to go before my shift ends. We'll be here when you get here!"

Before I finished my work, I had to call Lilac. I had planned on heading out early today so we could go to the circus. It was only in our town for a week, and Lilac really wanted to go. Yes, we had towns in Hell. It wasn't all just one area. It was very similar to Earth.

I knew she'd understand. After I took Gusion down to the dungeon the night of the dinner and concert, we finished our date. During that time, we spoke a lot about Gusion. Since her mother and father were both originals, she knew the betrayal we all felt when another original deceived us. Especially since, when she was a kid, she had an issue with Tempest because she had to spend time in Purgatory to see her mom.

Tempest took her on a weekend trip to the islands in Hell to get it all out because she hated the idea of Lilac being upset with her. By the time they got back, Lilac understood things a lot better, and she and Tempest had an amazing relationship.

I reluctantly grabbed the phone to call her. I wasn't hesitant because I thought she would be upset. Like I said, I knew she'd understand. No, it wasn't that. I was reluctant because I hated the idea of canceling a date with her. Spending every minute possible with her was my goal. But I didn't plan on canceling it. I hoped that Gusion and I would finish talking early enough so that Lilac and I could go to the circus tonight. Things stayed open longer in Hell than on Earth, so we had plenty of time.

She answered the call on the first ring. I couldn't help but hope that was because it was me calling. "Hey Don, what's up? You're not canceling our date now, are you?"

Of course, she had to answer the phone that way.

"I'm so sorry, Lilac. Hopefully, I'm not canceling and just putting it off until later. Ruby called me to let me know that Gusian asked to speak to me outside of the dungeon. Tempest had a feeling he would ask this, so she permitted Ruby to say yes before she left for Earth. If I'm being honest, I'm not looking forward to this at all. I know where he wants to go, and that will make the conversation worse."

"Oh, honey. Of course, we can postpone our date. If you end up needing to cancel, that will be fine. The circus is in town for four more days. This is more important than the circus. Call me when you're done, and we can make plans then. I know this is going to be emotional for you, so if you need to, we can cancel going to the circus and spend time together talking or whatever you need."

I knew this woman was the one for me for the last three years, but I did not know just how right for me she would be. I was quickly falling in love with her, which didn't surprise me.

"Thank you, Lilac. That sounds like a plan. I have a feeling that whatever we do, what will be most important is spending some time with you. You have a way about you that calms this old Demon."

She chuckled. "You may be an old Demon, but you're my old Demon." I never thought words could make me so happy until that moment.

"I can see that crimson blush climbing up your beautiful face. Just so you know, young Demon, you're mine, too." I thought I heard her sigh, but it was so soft I wasn't sure.

"I like that, old Demon. Now go do what you need to do so we can spend some time together. I love you." She didn't give me a chance to respond. She hung up as soon as the words were out of her mouth. Her words shouldn't have been a shock. Every time I looked into her eyes, I could see the love. But they did shock me... in the best way possible.

Screw working! I needed to see my Demon, so I had to get this meeting with Gusion done. I quickly headed down to the dungeon, and when I walked in the door to the guard's office, Ruby looked up from some paperwork. "You're early. I'm glad. Gusion has been pacing his cell. I think he needs this, Abaddon. I know he betrayed us all and doesn't deserve our sympathy, but we've been doing a lot of talking. It's not as simple as betraying us. Please hear him out."

CHAPTER THIRTEEN

discussions, discussions, discussions

"I'LL HEAR HIM OUT, Ruby. I would have done that, anyway. He doesn't deserve it after what he did. However, he is one of my oldest friends, and I need to hear him out as much as he needs me to hear him out. If not more so. I need to know why he would betray us all like this. If it was all worth it."

Ruby looked at me with sympathy on her face. "I understand, Don. I truly do. That's exactly how I feel. Still do, to some extent. I think he could have done things differently. He felt he had no other way. Just trust me when I say it wasn't what we think it was." I nodded at her as she handed me the keys to Gusion's cell.

I didn't think I could have walked any slower to the cell, which was just down the hall from the guard's office. When I got close, I could see Guison pacing. My former friend was as nervous as I was about this meeting. I didn't know why. It was his fault that we were in this predicament. He stopped pacing as soon as he heard me. He was facing away from me but stopped pacing, and his back stiffened.

70

After all our years of friendship, I was sure he recognized my footsteps.

When I got to the cell bars, I unlocked them slowly. I was desperately trying to prolong this. Once it was open, I went into the cell and removed the handcuffs from my belt. I walked over to Gusion and grabbed his wrists to put them on him. I knew some Demons, hell, some humans, who would have been rough in doing so, but I couldn't do that. No matter what he had done, I couldn't let go of our friendship. Some Demons could turn feelings on and off like a water faucet, but I was unable to do that. I'd never been that Demon.

"Gusion, Ruby tells me I can take you out of the dungeon to talk. She also told me you have someplace specific in mind. Do I even need to ask where that is?" The look on his face almost brought me to my knees. He was a broken man.

"No, I don't think you have to ask, Abby." I know. I told Ruby not to call me that. And almost no one could. The only one who could get away with that is Gusion. If anyone else was in his position right now, with me holding all the cards, it wouldn't end well. No matter what had happened, I couldn't find it in me to say anything about it.

"The top cliff on the other side of the castle it is. Are those too tight? If you'd like, I'll loosen them." I hated even giving that option. I'd never done it before, no matter who the prisoner was.

"They're fine, Abby. I'd just love to get out in the sunshine. I know it's been only a couple of days, but not going outside is tough. When you talk to Tempest, can you thank her for allowing us to go outside? I know we could talk in here, but I miss being able to go outside." Gusion loved sunshine, so this had to be hard on him.

"There's a way that you could have avoided all of this. A way that you could have been out as often as you wanted. You went the other route." Gusion sighed as I grabbed his arm, and we walked out of the cell.

"I promise I'm going to explain it all, Abby. I have nothing to lose at this point. He can't hurt me now." I jerked my head in his direction. A chill came over me as I wondered what he was talking about.

"What does that mean? Who are you talking about?" He tried to keep walking while I tried to stay there.

"Like I said, I'll explain it all. Can we just get out of here first?" I continued walking, and when we got to the guard's office, we went in so I could give Ruby the keys.

Ruby looked at our friend with tears in her eyes. What the fuck was going on here? "It's going to be okay, Gusion. Explain everything to Don, and then we'll all go talk to Tempest when she and Jacob return. Have faith that it will all work out."

Gusion just nodded his head, yes, and we walked out of the office. The top cliff on the other side of the castle wasn't too close to the dungeon area, but we both needed the air and time to think. Neither of us spoke as we walked to the cliff's edge.

Once we got to the cliff, I took the handcuffs off my friend. Something told me it was okay. We both then sat on the tree stumps we had been sitting on since we were all creating Hell. We'd always gone to this place when we wanted to talk to each other without being interrupted. That's how I knew this was the place that Gusion would want to go to have this discussion. I was the first to speak. "Ruby tells me that there is more to this story, and between your comment in the cell and Ruby having tears in her eyes when she saw you in cuffs, I know that there is a lot that I don't know."

"I don't even know where to begin, Abby. You're right. There is a lot that you don't know. I guess the beginning would be a good start. About a year ago, the leader of the opposition came to me. He wants Tempest's power badly. At first, he tried to be friends with me. Of course, that didn't work. He tried for a couple of months before he went to threats. Knowing I'm much more powerful than him, he knew it couldn't be just any threat. It had to be something big. He also knew he had to go further than a threat. If he just threatened me, I would take care of it. But he took it further."

Gusion took a minute to breathe, and I waited for him to continue. I didn't want to rush him, knowing he needed to get this out. "There was something I had told no one yet. It was something new, and we weren't ready to share the information with anyone yet." We? Who was 'we'? Who was he talking about?

"About four months before he came to me, I had found my one true mate. She's not from around this part of Hell, and no one around here has met her. I had traveled one day to one of the outer cities, and that's when we met. She's so beautiful, Abby. Her name is Kali. She has long blonde hair and the greenest eyes I have ever seen. I love her, Abby, more than I thought possible."

I was glad he was still speaking, as I didn't know what to say. "When I wouldn't willingly join him, he started with vague threats against Kali. Nothing concrete I could fight back against. He also told me if I went to anyone, he would kill her. I decided I would bring her here in the middle of the night. Only I didn't get there quick enough. When I got to her house, her mother was hysterical. The bastard had been there less than a half hour earlier and had taken her. Eventually, he contacted me and told me I would never see her again unless I joined his side. He also told me I would not get her back until I helped to defeat Tempest. He still has her."

It seemed he had gotten it all out, and I didn't know what to say. "I'm not sure how we'll fix this. However, we'll find a way. I promise, Gusion. Tempest is due back tomorrow, and, like Ruby said, the three of us will talk to her. You know Tempest as well as I do, so you know what she'll say. We'll fix this, Gusion, and we'll bring Kali back to you. The best plan may be to keep you in the dungeon and let them think we don't know the truth, but we'll come up with a solid plan. I need to go talk to my Demon. Yes, Lilac finally gave in to my sorry ass. We'll talk more about that later. I'm going to take you back to the dungeon, and we'll talk to Tempest tomorrow. We'll get her back, my friend." We walked back to the dungeon quicker, with the handcuffs still in my belt. Ruby had a huge smile on her face when we walked in, and she saw there were no handcuffs.

"We're going to fix this, Ruby, but until we come up with a plan, we need Gusion in a cell. We want everyone to think that he's still in custody. Make sure he has everything he needs, though. And no dungeon food. I need to go talk to Lilac now. When Tempest and Jacob return, I'll set up a time for us all to speak."

I didn't even call Lilac. Instead, I went straight to her house. She came to the door quickly when she heard me banging on it. As soon as she opened it, I grabbed her in my arms and kissed her with all my love for her. When I finally put her down, she started giggling. "What did I do to deserve that?"

"You're you, that's what you did. You're the Demon I have fallen completely and totally in love with. Hearing you tell me you love me today made me realize I wasn't only falling in love with you. I'm deeply in love with you."

She pulled me in the door and shut it quietly. Once we were both inside, she looked up at me. "Are you sure, Don?"

I grabbed her in my arms again. "Baby, I've never been sure of anything in my life."

CHAPTER FOURTEEN

tempest and jacob return to hell

ON THE FIRST night we spent at Jacob's parents' house, his mother planned a family dinner. She knew we wouldn't be staying long, and although Jacob would be able to visit whenever he wanted, we didn't know when I would be able to return. His mom wanted his brothers to meet me.

His mom's cooking was better than any of the chefs in Hell, and that was saying a lot. We had some of the best. His brothers were already there when we got downstairs after a short rest. I could tell which one was Justin and which was James as soon as I saw them from having seen their pictures.

Justin came over and shook my hand as soon as he saw me. James, on the other hand, glared at me from the couch. "Tempest, it's nice to meet you. I'm sure you understand how much of a surprise all of this is. Honestly, it was a lot to take in. But my brother's happiness is what matters to me."

"Justin, it's great to meet you, also. I understand completely. Trust me, none of this was what I expected, either. Your brother's happiness is very important to me, too, and I'm going to do everything in my power to make him happy."

I noticed his mom looking at James, and she didn't seem very happy. "James, do you have a problem? Why are you looking at Tempest like that? There is no reason for it. "

James was quick to respond. "No reason for it? My baby brother brings home Satan and says she's his mate, and there's no reason to have a problem with it? Have you all lost your minds? She is Satan. The very definition of evil. How can you all accept this?"

Their father started to respond, but I asked him not to. I wanted to address James' concerns. "James, you have valid reasons for your concerns. Humans know very little about me, and what little you do know isn't good. Most of the stories about me aren't true; however, I know it may be easier for me to say that than for you to believe it. It's only been a couple of days, but your brother already means the world to me. Fate never gets one's true mate wrong. Jacob and I are meant to be together. While I don't ask you to accept me at this moment, I do ask that you give me a chance."

He didn't look sure about this, but he got up and came over to shake my hand. "I still have reservations about this, Tempest, but I will do what you ask and give you a chance. Like Justin, my brother's happiness is what's most important to me here. If you can make him happy, I don't care who you are. I apologize for my attitude."

Jacob walked over to us and hugged his brother. "Thank you, James. She does make me happy, more than you could ever know. Once you get to know her, you'll understand how wrong most of the stories we grew up hearing were. So very wrong."

Once the initial-awkwardness was over, we spent a nice evening together. Although I could still sense some reluctance on James' part, he was starting to come around by the end of the night.

Jacob lived in the same city as one of my long-time friends, Beatrix. Beatrix was a vampire and one of the sweetest people I know. I would never tell her that, though. We'd been friends with benefits several times over the years, but we both knew we were better as friends. She also never gave up on meeting her one true mate, and I didn't think she would ever get serious about anyone until she did.

It had been about five years since we last saw each other, so Jacob and I planned a quick visit before we left. The rest of the time would be spent with his family so we could all get to know each other better.

After spending a week on earth, it was time to go back to Hell. Last night, I received a text from Abaddon informing me of a recent development with the Gusion situation. He said little more than that, but I believed it was big.

Jacob's mom and dad were going to go back with us to see their son's new home, but we talked them out of it. They were nervous about Jacob living in Hell, but they also knew it wasn't their decision to make. We both understood their feelings and wouldn't try to push them into being okay with it. We had many pictures from Hell on our phones, which helped convince them they could put off their trip while Jacob and I dealt with the issues there.

We knew they'd be visiting eventually, so I was going to get a wing in the castle prepared for them. After spending the last few days together, I had gotten to know them well, so I had a good idea of what would make them comfortable. My staff could get anything I put on the list right in Hell, but if not, my staff always love to go on shopping trips topside. This means finding someone to get what's needed won't be difficult.

Jacob brought a lot of stuff back with us; we would have Blade pick up the rest of his belongings. It was all at the parent's house, in one room, and packed up. This would make it easy for him to pick it up. While there, I spoke to Blade, who told me he and Kishi realized they were true mates.

I was going to give them both a two-week paid vacation on Earth, with all expenses paid. In the end, they'd pick up Jacob's things and come back to Hell. It will be a win-win for everyone, and

Blade loved the idea. He couldn't wait to explore Earth with Kishi, even for a short time.

When we got to the portal in the garden, staff were waiting for us to help bring Jacob's things up to our quarters. I liked to travel, but coming home was always a good feeling. Jacob and I helped bring his things upstairs, as it wasn't fair to make the staff do all of it while we did none. Just because I was Satan didn't mean I couldn't be fair and take care of those who took care of me and those closest to me. I had a very dedicated staff, and they deserved no less.

After we got everything up to our quarters, I called Abaddon to see if he had time to meet with me so we could discuss the recent developments with Gusion. He must have seen us come home because he said he was already in my office.

I let him know I would be down in a few minutes and called out to Jacob. "Hey, baby. I just got off the phone with Abaddon. I'm going to head down to my office to talk to him about whatever happened with Gusion. You can stay here and put your stuff away or join us in the meeting since you'll be running Hell by my side one day."

I walked into our bedroom before I finished. "To be honest, I'd rather you come with me. I don't want to put off making sure that people know your position. I don't expect there will be a problem, but I want people to get used to you being by my side in personal and business matters."

Jacob grabbed me by my waist and kissed me before responding. As usual, his kiss almost made me forget what we were talking about. "Of course, I'll go with you, my beauty. I think that's the best way to handle it, too."

We could handle putting his things away later. Now, it was time to handle business. "Let's go then, Mr. Satan!" Jacob chuckled and slapped my ass.

Abaddon didn't seem shocked that Jacob was with me when we got to my office. He got up to say hi and shook both of our hands. "It's nice to see you both back. I hope you had a great time topside.

Since Jacob is here, I'm guessing he is going to start his new role helping you run this place."

I smiled at one of my oldest friends. He was always so accepting of everything I did, even when he knew something was not my smartest idea. I knew that having Jacob by my side was the best move I had made in a long time. If not, the smartest ever.

We all quickly sat down so I could find out what was going on. "What did you learn, Don? It seemed like it was critical information."

Abaddon nodded his head yes. "It is, Tempest. I would rather Gusion tell you the story, though. It is his story to tell, not mine. Do you both have time to go down to the dungeons now?"

Now, I was perplexed. Why did he want me to hear the story from Gusion himself? "Of course, Don. Do we have to call down, or will they be expecting us?"

"Ruby is on duty, and she's expecting us. She knew you were coming back, and I told her we would hopefully be down there sometime today."

When we all walked to my office door, I noticed Abaddon appeared stressed. I took hold of Jacob's hand so he could help me stay calm. This whole situation had me concerned.

When we got to the guard's office in the dungeon, I noticed an extra guard. Usually, when Ruby was on shift, she was the only guard. She could handle most of the Demons in Hell, so she was the only guard needed. As we walked in, both stood up, and the other guard, Damian, bowed. "Damian, I've told you many times that you don't have to bow. I'm your boss, not your queen. Please stand."

The young Demon stood up and smiled. "Thank you, Satan. I'll try to remember."

I looked over at Ruby when she cleared her throat. "Tempest, I asked Damien to be here so he can monitor things while we all go to another office to speak. I hope that is okay." Hmmm... even Ruby was going to be there for this conversation.

"You know I trust your judgment, Ruby. That's fine. How about we get Gusion out of his cell and go to my office in the back? It's the biggest office down here, with the most seats."

When we got close to Gusion's cell, I noticed he was pacing. As soon as he heard our footsteps, he stopped and looked up at us. Some might think it was crazy having Jacob with us since he was a human and Gusion had turned to the enemy. However, I had a feeling it would be safe. And if it wasn't Abaddon, Ruby and I could handle the situation. "Tempest, it's good to have you back. Jacob, it's nice to meet you, but I wish it were under different circumstances." I was sure he did.

"Gusion, we're going to let you out and go to my office. Do we need to cuff you?" Abaddon was the one who responded.

"I can assure you it will be fine, Tempest. You know I wouldn't do anything to put you or Jacob in danger." That I did not doubt. "Okay, Ruby, do you have the key?"

Ruby stepped forward and opened the bars. When Gusion stepped out, she hugged him, and I could hear her tell him that everything would be fine. Abaddon and Ruby were not acting like people whom Gusion had betrayed.

Once we got to my office, we all took our seats. We sat in the chairs surrounding the coffee table. It didn't feel like a situation where I needed to be formal and sit at my desk. I asked if anyone wanted anything to drink, but they said they just wanted to begin. Just one more thing that made me think that I'm going to need a drink, but I didn't say that. Jacob sat in the chair closest to me, and we each reached over so we could hold hands. "Gusion, Abaddon told me it would be better if I heard the story from you. He told me it's your story to tell. Would you care to begin?"

When he began, he asked me a favor. "Can I ask you not to say anything until I finish? I know I don't have the right to ask for favors, but it will make this easier."

I nodded my head yes and waited for him to continue.

"He came to me almost a year ago, pretending to be my friend. I've always been loyal to you, Tempest, and the rest of the originals, and it broke my heart to do anything different. For a couple of months, he tried to be friends with me, but when that didn't work, he began making threats. Eventually, he realized it would take more than a threat to make me turn to his side. I'm more powerful than he is and could handle a threat from the likes of him."

He took a breath before continuing. I didn't like the sound of this at all. "I had been keeping a secret. About four months before he came to me, I found my true mate. We kept it secret, but somehow, he found out. She's from one of the outer cities, so it was easy to keep her a secret. Or so I thought. Her name is Kali, and she is beautiful."

I didn't like the sound of this.

"He stepped it up. In the beginning, it was a vague threat. Nothing that I could fight back against. He told me if I told anyone, he would kill her. Understand, I couldn't take a chance. I went and got her in the middle of the night to bring her here. When I got there, her mom was hysterical. She said he had been there less than half an hour before and had taken Kali. He told me I would not get her back until I helped him defeat Tempest. He still has her."

After standing up, I walked over to him. Pulling him up from his seat, I hugged him, my heart breaking for him. "I'm so sorry, Gusion." I wanted to cry for him. Yes, Satan cried occasionally. "We'll get her back. She'll be back to you soon, okay?" He looked at me with tears in his eyes and shook his head. "I think the best thing is for you to stay in the dungeon for now. We don't want him to know that you've told us any of this. I promise you, we'll come up with a plan and bring Kali back to you. We're also going to take him and his army down."

Gusion shook his head. "He doesn't have an army, Tempest. I mean, he does, but they're all there for the same reason I was. He forced them all. So, I don't think it will be hard to take him down because I don't think he'll have any backup."

I saw Abaddon's eyes shine silver, his Demon within close to the surface. "Even better. Don't worry, Gusion. Kali will be back with you before you know it. And he's going to be one dead Demon."

CHAPTER FIFTEEN

jacob's parents visit early

JACOB and I had a lot going on between working on a plan to flush out the opposition leader and saving Gusion's mate, Kali. A lot was riding on this. We would finally put a stop to the latest coup attempts, and Gusion would have his mate by his side. We could not lose; the stakes were too high.

That was why we were very careful in devising a plan. It helped that Gusion knew who the leader was. This put us ahead of the game, even if it was only a fraction ahead of our opponent. Although a fraction was better than nothing, we still needed a foolproof plan, and we felt we had that.

Bastien was one of the Demons that jumped with us. While I always knew he resented me for what happened, I never thought he was the one trying to unseat me. Although the other Demons that jumped when I did were happy with the life we created, Bastien was not. He also didn't feel that he could ever return to Heaven, even after God made that a possibility. He'd lived his life to be angry at me —that I always knew. We figured out that even though the Demons involved couldn't tell us anything by speaking, they could write down what they knew. So Gusion was finally able to tell us who it was. The witch working for Bastien was stupider than we initially thought. If she had done the spell right, no one would have been about to tell us anything by any means.

Knowing who it was made ending this so much easier. One of the reasons we had such a hard time ending this situation was we didn't know where they were hiding out. Hell was vast, and finding people who wanted to hide was difficult. Years ago, Bastien had moved to a desolate area of the northwestern edge of Hell that we were unable to build on.

I always hated him deciding to move there. I had no idea how he was surviving. No matter what I did to convince him to move to another part of Hell, he wouldn't do it. This explained why. I didn't know exactly how long he had been planning this, but I suspected it was much longer than we knew.

An elite set of guards, led by Abaddon and Blade, would infiltrate his camp. We knew enough to determine the exact time that would work best. We also knew all we needed to do was catch Bastien since he had blackmailed all of the people working for him into doing so.

I knew it was hard for Gusion to still be in the cell in the dungeon, especially knowing he was innocent. However, having met Jacob and knowing the true mate pull, I knew not having Kali by his side was even more challenging. Knowing that she was being held captive has to be killing him inside.

Jacob and I had been back for two days and hadn't stopped since we returned. Not only did I have to work, but we wanted to be sure that Jacob learned the inner workings of both Hell and my job running the place. The added pressure of working on a plan to find Bastien made everything busier than ever.

We'd been up for about an hour, and I was in my office discussing viable plans of action with my top generals while Jacob was down in the dungeon learning how we run it. The Demon who oversaw the dungeons had decided it was time to retire, and Jacob didn't want to spend his time down here as only my mate, so he would take over running the dungeons when Mantus left. Mantus was still young, at least in Demon years, but he also recently met his one true mate, and they decided they wanted to do some traveling on Earth.

We were getting frustrated in my office, unable to come to a consensus on how we wanted to handle things. The only thing we could agree on was the elite guard going in there. But we needed more than that. And we needed it quickly. Suddenly, we heard a sharp knock at the door, and Jacob walked into my office.

"Hey, baby, what's up? Are you taking a break from the dungeons?" I could tell by the look on my mate's face that he felt stressed, so I looked at my generals and asked them to give us a few minutes. They quickly got up and left.

"We have a problem. Nothing like what we're currently dealing with, but a problem." That was all we needed, another problem.

"Should I be concerned?" I asked, knowing the answer was probably yes.

"I don't think it's anything to be too concerned about, but it's not what we planned on. My mom just called me. Blade went by their house, and my dad gave them the house keys so they would get my stuff." I wasn't sure what the problem could be. Maybe they were planning a vacation. *Oh no. No, no, no. That can't be it.*

"Jacob, don't tell me they're coming for a visit. Please don't tell me that." The look on his face said it all. We were expecting a visit from my future in-laws.

"I tried everything, Tempest. Nothing I said could convince my mom that it was not a good time for a visit. The one situation that may convince her is not something I can tell her. I mean, how do I tell my human mother that we're trying to devise a plan to defeat a Demon trying to take you down?"

Like Jacob, I thought that instead of deterring her, that would cause her to travel down right now. If she believed Jacob was in danger, which he wasn't, she would be down here right away.

"Well, there's not a lot we can do about it. I told them where the closest portal to Hell was and gave each of them a charm to use it. At least this way, we'll know when they are coming so someone can wait for them at the portal in the garden. I'm afraid they will just show up if we tell them they can't come."

Jacob didn't look happy. "I am 100% positive that's what would happen. My mom can be stubborn; if we tell them no, they will still show up. Keeping them safe is important. I won't have my parents hurt because of me."

I couldn't agree with him more. First, they were Jacob's parents. I never wanted to see him hurt. There was also the fact that I'd gotten to know them well, and they were going to be my in-laws. It had been years since I'd had parental figures in my life, and I'd be damned if I allowed anything to happen to them.

"They'll be fine, Jacob. I'll put the word out with all the guards that they are to be protected as they protect us. Blade will guard their suite. We'll put them in the suite with no outside door and on the top floor so no one will get in by the windows. We'll keep them safe. There is no one better than Blade. Even Abaddon, as good as he is at so many things, is not as good of a guard as Blade."

I walked over to my mate and put my arms around him. I thought we could both use the calming effect that touching each other had on us both. "When will they be here? Please tell me we have a day or even two." We could get prepared in one day; however, two would be better.

"It's better than that. They'll be coming on Friday, and today is only Tuesday."

I took a deep breath. That was a relief. Having them here when all of this was happening was still not ideal, but at least we had enough time to prepare.

"That's longer than I expected. I love your parents, but we both know how impulsive your mom can be. I'm surprised they didn't call us from the portal in the garden."

Jacob chuckled. Mostly because he knew I was right.

Then he got serious. "We'll be able to keep them safe, right?" I looked into those beautiful eyes that I love so much.

"I'm Satan, remember? I can make sure everyone is safe. Seri-ously, love, they'll be fine. I'll make sure no harm comes to them. They know we must work, so they won't suspect anything is up. We'll set up a guard team for when they want to go out and do touristy stuff around Hell. We want them to be comfortable here. That means they need to get to know Hell and our people."

CHAPTER SIXTEEN

abaddon and lilac visit lilith

IT HAD ONLY BEEN a couple of weeks since Lilac finally realized I was her mate. She had been asking me to go to Purgatory to see Lilith almost since day one. She said Lilith was happy for us and just wanted to spend some time with us.

The problem was that Lilac tried to see only the best in her mother. I had known her mother since we were both children and angels in Heaven, before we all fell or jumped, depending on the story you believed. I knew her mother too well to think that she only wanted to spend time with us.

One reason I believed her was it was very hard for Demons to lie to their mates. But more important than that, Lilac wasn't like other Demons. Lilac was the epitome of good. Lying wasn't something she did at all, never mind lying to her mate. Honestly, I didn't care why she didn't realize it sooner. I was just grateful that she had realized it now.

It had been crazy down in Hell since we got together, so putting off going to Purgatory has been easy. It's still crazy down in Hell, so it should have been easy for me to continue to put it off, at least for the foreseeable future. If Tempest hadn't given me a week's vacation.

I was pretty sure Lilac finally gave up on my agreeing to go to Purgatory and went to Tempest to ask for her help. We'd been working on a plan to capture the leader of the opposition, therefore saving Gusion's mate and allowing him to get out of the dungeon, finally, for almost three weeks. I knew this was not a decision that Satan would have made on her own.

There was nothing I could do. Tempest not only told me I could have a week's vacation to visit Lilith in Purgatory, but she also told me she "insisted on it." That was Satan-speak for saying I had no choice.

I understood why. It wasn't just to make Lilac happy. Although that played into it, I was sure. Tempest seemed to really like Lilac. Tempest also wanted to make Lilith happy. Not that she cared if Lilith was happy, but she was hoping if Lilith was happy, she'd behave so that the council would finally allow her to return to Hell.

People thought Tempest had no heart—especially the humans who lived topside. The fact of the matter was she had an enormous heart. Ever since Lilac turned 18 and lived full-time in Hell, Tempest had hated that she must live without her mother. That she was the one to send Lilith to Purgatory made her feel even worse.

She also knew that having my future mother-in-law living in Hell would drive me crazy. Lilith never passed up an opportunity to drive me crazy. I was all packed, and Lilac was going to meet me at the castle since the closest portal to us both was in the castle garden. I was just about to call her when I heard a knock at my door. "That must be her." I wasn't sure who I was talking to.

When I opened the door, Lilac's beauty took my breath away. She had always been beautiful, but she was breathtaking tonight. Her curly blonde hair flowed down her back to her waist. She wore tight black jeans with a white off-the-shoulder cashmere sweater that looked as soft as an angel's wings and completed her outfit with black thigh-high boots.

"Lilac..." I didn't get to finish my thought because she jumped in my arms and kissed me roughly, her tongue seeking entrance to my mouth. We stood at my door, her in my arms, kissing fervently until we heard someone cough behind us.

I slowly opened one eye, still kissing my mate, to see who was behind us. Of course. It was Tempest. I should have known. No one else would have the guts to pull such a stunt. I gently disengaged from Lilac and put her back on the floor. She slowly turned around. I was sure she hoped she wasn't right about who it was. She bowed as soon as she saw Tempest. "I'm so sorry, Satan. That wasn't very becoming."

"Lilac, how many times do I have to tell you I don't like it when people bow to me? Especially the child of one of my oldest friends, no matter how crazy she drives me. It makes me itch. There is nothing wrong with what you and Abaddon were doing. I've done the same thing myself, once or a thousand times. I just wanted to see if either of you needs anything before your trip. Are you leaving today"

I shook my head at my boss and closest friend. "We are leaving as soon as you leave my suite. Is that soon enough?"

Lilac gasped. Most Demons weren't used to Demons talking to Satan that way. She should see her mother and Tempest together. She'd probably learn a few extra words. "I don't think we need anything. I'm all packed, and Lilac keeps extras of everything she'll need in Purgatory for when she visits her mother. So, we're good to go."

"Do you need someone to help with your luggage? I can have someone come up."

She wanted us to get going. I was going to get even with her for this one day. "We're only going to be gone a week, Tempest. I don't have that much luggage. I can carry it down to the garden."

Once Tempest finally left us alone, we went into my suite so I could grab my luggage. Lilac jumped back in my arms and tried to resume what we were doing before Tempest interrupted us, but I knew we would never leave if we went down that path.

"Baby, I would love to finish what we started, but that will end up with us in my bedroom, not Purgatory. Both your mother and Tempest would blame me for that, and I'm not having those two Demons mad at me."

She pulled away from me, pouting. "I know you're right. It's just hard for me to keep my hands off you."

"Well, look at me. I'm a God. Of course it's hard to keep your hands off me."

She smirked at me. "A God? Really, Demon? You sure you don't want to change your wording?"

She was feisty when she wanted to be. Something this old Demon needed. I'd always loved a feisty woman. I gave Lilac my keys so she could lock the door and grabbed my luggage. Why did I feel like I was about to meet my doom?

CHAPTER SEVENTEEN

lilac is done with lilith

IT TOOK us no time at all to arrive. Purgatory wasn't as bland as it once was, thanks to Tempest redecorating about ten years ago, but it still sucked. Instead of leaving the whole place white, Tempest added some pink to the mix. Even all the houses were painted white and pink, not only the buildings that were Purgatory property. No, every damn building was pink and white. It made my eyes bleed.

Lilith was there as soon as we stepped out of the portal. I knew Lilac had called her to let her know we were coming, but I didn't expect her to be waiting for us. The look on her face told me she was not happy to see me.

"Lilac!! And *Abaddon*."

Her tone when she said my name showed her true feelings. Venom dripped from her voice as she said it. No matter what she'd been saying, she loathed me being her daughter's mate. She'd never had a problem with me before; in fact, we'd always been friends, even after she was sent to Purgatory. Or so I thought. I was sure this change in attitude was because I was Lilac's mate. Well, this should be fun!

I looked at my mate. The look on her face told me she was not happy. When I heard Lilith's tone, I was afraid it would upset Lilac, but it seemed to have pissed her off. This was going to be interesting. Lilac was very sweet, but I'd also seen her strength over the past couple of weeks. Lilith looked shocked, so I didn't think she expected this side of her daughter, either.

"Lilith, it's good to see you again. Thanks for meeting us." I didn't want to kiss her ass, but I wasn't sure that I had any choice. I knew Lilac loved me, and since she was my mate, Lilith could never come between us. However, she was still Lilac's mother. If she wasn't, she would have found herself in the Purgatory dungeon right now, and she knew it.

"Don't talk to me, Demon. You're one of my oldest friends. We fell together from Heaven, and you do this to me?"

Lilac was tired of hearing her mother speak. "Shut up now, Mother! You know as well as we do that Fate and Destiny choose people's mates. They are also two of your oldest friends. Maybe if you ever get out of Purgatory, God will let you into Heaven, and you can speak to them. Until then, just *shut up*. Abaddon is my mate. Period."

Lilith looked like she was going to have a heart attack. She sputtered. I was sure Lilac had never spoken to her like that before. It took her a few minutes before she could respond to her daughter coherently. "Don't you ever talk to me like that again, Lilac. I'm your mother."

"I am your daughter, and Abaddon is my mate. You will respect us both. If you can't do that, Abaddon and I will spend all our time in Hell. If we do that, you will never see me again, which will mean you will never see your grandchildren when we have kids. It's your choice."

Hearing Lilac speak about our future children made me happier than I ever thought I could be. However, before we could think about our future, we needed to finish this visit. With all three of us alive. Although it was incredibly hard to kill Demons, especially Demons like Lilith and myself, who were among the original Demons, I knew we could make it happen.

"Ladies, this isn't solving anything. Lilith, how about we go to your home? No one needs to see us air our family laundry." I knew that would make her angry. I simply didn't care.

"Don't you *dare* say 'our family.' You are not, and will never be, a part of my family."

I wasn't sure why she was pushing this. Lilac had already made her feelings clear. Lilith loved all her daughters and would never want to hurt them. Lilith and I had been friends our whole lives. I couldn't fathom why she was acting this way. I knew I was much older than Lilac, but several of Lilith's daughters had mated with original Demons. So, I knew that wasn't it. There had been nothing remotely romantic between Lilith and me, so I also knew she didn't want me for herself. Whatever her reason was, she needed to get over it.

As soon as I heard my mother's tone when she said Abaddon's name, I knew that this visit simply would not work for me. But since we were here, we might as well have this out. "Mother, Abaddon is right. We don't need to be airing our dirty laundry in front of the portal like this. A lot of Demons are milling about."

"Our dirty laundry? The only thing dirty here is this Demon that you're claiming is your mate. I told him as soon as he came to me when you turned 18 that I would never allow this to happen. I don't give a damn what Fate and Destiny decided. He will **NOT** be your mate. Do you hear me, Lilac? Now he can go back to Hell, alone, and you are moving back here to Purgatory."

She was insane if she thought either of those things was happening. I could tell by Abaddon's growling that he wouldn't allow it, either. "Mother, I don't know what your problem is, and frankly, I don't care. He is **NOT** going back to Hell alone, and I am **NOT** moving back to Purgatory. I am 20 years old, and you have no say over what I do with my life. Make no mistake about that."

I looked over at my mate because his growling was intensifying. The first thing I noticed when I looked at him was his eyes. They were blood red. If I didn't calm him down, this was going to quickly get violent. "Abaddon, I got this. Calm down, baby." I took one of his hands in my hands, and he visibly calmed down, his eyes returning to their normal color. "We can either go back to your house to discuss this, or Abaddon and I can go right back through the portal. That's your two choices. Just remember, I **WILL** go back to Hell with my mate."

She looked at me like I'd lost my mind. She probably thought I had since I've never spoken to her like that in the past. "Lilac, you will not speak to me like that. We can go back to my house to discuss this, but I will not change my mind. In the end, you'll have a choice to make. Me or him. Be sure when you make that choice. You won't be able to undo it."

I couldn't believe she was taking things this far. It wouldn't change anything, though. If she made me choose between her and Abaddon, I would choose Abaddon every time. I took hold of my mate's hand, planning on walking to my mom's house. It was less than two blocks away from the portal.

We were about to go when we suddenly found ourselves in my mother's living room. What the actual fuck, Mother! Since when do you have magic? How were you able to do that?"

She shrugged her shoulders. "There's a lot you don't know, Lilac. How I have magic isn't important. You two take a seat. I need to go make a phone call. I'll be back in a few minutes. Stay here."

Once my mother was gone, Abaddon and I looked at each other. I could understand her telling Abaddon to stay here with how she acted, but this was my childhood home. There was no reason for her to tell me to stay here. Abaddon started to speak, but I looked at him and shook my head. I pointed to the couch, letting him know I wanted him to take a seat.

Once he sat down, I used our telepathy to let him know what I was doing. "Something is going on here. I'm going to find her and listen to that conversation. She told me to stay here when there is no need to, so I have a feeling the conversation she is having has to do with us."

Telepathy was something that all mates shared. At least all Demon mates. I'd never been sure about other supernaturals. This situation made me realize how much it can come in handy. I didn't want my mother to know I was coming her way.

"I'm not sure about this, Lilac. We don't know what's going on." I heard my mate's voice in my head. While I understood his concern, we had to know what my mother was up to. It might have had to do with why I didn't feel the mating pull earlier.

"She would never hurt me, no matter what this is about. We both know this. I'm going to turn on the TV to make her think we're watching it, then I'm going to find her."

I turned on the TV and quietly headed in the direction that my mother had gone. Something was going on here, and I was going to find out what it was. I noticed the door to her office was almost completely closed except for a tiny crack. I heard her voice coming through from the other side.

I sauntered to the door, standing behind it so she wouldn't see me through the gap. It was tiny, but all Demons had very good eyesight. I was close enough to hear her breathing heavily. She was not happy with whomever she was talking to.

Finally, she spoke. "Why didn't the spell to keep the mating pull hidden from my daughter work? I will not have her mated with that Demon. He helped Tempest have me thrown down here. You screwed this up. You need to fix it!"

I had heard enough. I called Abaddon through our connection. "Get to my mother's office. *NOW*!"

I pushed open the door and entered my mother's office. I could hear Abaddon running down the hall. "Who do you think you are, Lilith? You used a spell to hide the mating pull from me? The decision to send you to Purgatory was Tempest's and hers alone, and you damn well know that! Abaddon had nothing to do with that!"

Abaddon was in the doorway, and I could tell he heard everything I said from his roar. She'd be lucky if he didn't tear her apart, and I wouldn't stop him. She tried to ruin my life because she broke laws and ended up in Purgatory? I always knew she wasn't the mother of the year, but I thought she was better than this.

"Lilac, you're overreacting. He doesn't deserve you and never will. Just let him go back to Hell, and you move back in here." She really was insane.

"I don't know what to say to you, Lilith. Oh wait, yes, I do. I'm done. Our relationship is over. I never want to see you again."

I walked over to Abaddon but turned around. "One more thing. As soon as we get back to Hell, we're going to talk to Tempest and tell her what you did. Abaddon is not only one of her top generals, but also one of her closest friends. You tried to ruin his life. You'll never get out of Purgatory now."

I walked over to Abaddon, and he picked me up and carried me as we left my mother's home for the last time. I would not be back. Hiding my face against my mate's shoulder, I cried quietly. I hated my mother for what she'd done, but she was still my mother. My decision to put her out of my life was the right one. I don't doubt that. That didn't mean it didn't cause me pain.

CHAPTER EIGHTEEN

abaddon and lilac
return to hell

WE LEFT Lilith's house as soon as Lilac finished telling her exactly what she thought of her for putting a spell on her so she wouldn't feel the mating pull. Lilac didn't seem to want to leave my arms, so I held her tight while we walked back to the portal.

Luckily, we left our luggage outside the portal instead of taking it back to Lilith's since we didn't know whether we were staying. Purgatory might be full of people being punished by Satan or God for something, but it was still very safe. People wanted out of Purgatory, so they didn't break the laws. Which meant our luggage was safe.

I kept one arm around Lilac while I used my other hand to carry the bags back into the portal. Once we got back to Hell, I telepathically asked Tempest to send someone to the portal to get our luggage and bring it back to my room. Lilac would stay with me until I moved into her home. Lilith still had allies in Hell.

I also asked Tempest to meet us at her office. "Tempest, is there any way you can meet us in your office to talk? There's something that we believe you should know." Tempest must have wondered what was going on because she answered me right away, just as an officer came through the door to get our luggage. She never answered right away.

"Of course, Abaddon. I'm guessing this has something to do with why you're back so soon. I'm in my office. Meet me here now." I immediately cut off our connection to talk to Lilac.

"Baby, can I put you down? If not, that's okay. I don't mind carrying you. I want to be sure that you're comfortable with me carrying you around Hell."

She sniffled softly, and one of her hands went to her eyes to wipe them. She had been quietly crying the whole way here. "You can put me down. Thank you for holding me. I know this shouldn't surprise me, but it does. How could she do this to her daughter? Not only would her actions eventually drive you crazy, but they would also have eventually driven me crazy. She knows even if someone doesn't recognize the mate pull, that's what happens."

I put my hand on her back as we started walking towards the castle. "If I'm being honest, I would have never expected this either. And I grew up with the woman, so I know what she is capable of. You've always been her favorite daughter, and you know there are a lot of you. I'm not surprised that she wanted to hurt me, since she blames me in part for Tempest putting her in Purgatory. But to hurt you? Never saw that coming."

We both stopped talking at that point, each deep in our own thoughts, while we walked to Tempest's office. Once we got there, the door was open. Tempest must have been curious about what was going on because she always shut her door when she was in there. She didn't like to be disturbed while working. She told us to go into her office right before we got to the door.

I sat on the couch as soon as we got to the office and pulled Lilac onto my lap. "You will not like this, Tempest. Lilith has not changed at all. Something needs to be done about her because she has gone too far this time. She's lucky I didn't kill her. I'll let Lilac explain what happened." The look on Satan's face said she was about to lose it. Wait until she heard what Lilith did.

I pulled myself together while Abaddon and I walked to Tempest's office. I had my time to cry. Now, I wanted something done. Not only would I never forgive my mother for what she did, but I also wanted her punished. And not one of Tempest's regular punishments, either. I wanted a proper punishment, one that would hurt her so much she wouldn't be able to come back from it.

"I don't even know how to say this, Satan..."

She interrupted me. "Call me Tempest, please. There is no reason to stand on formality. You are the mate of one of my closest friends, and that makes you my friend, too. I'm sorry I interrupted you. Please continue."

"Thank you, Tempest. I'm not going into the entire story of how we found this out. I'm just going to say what we learned. Kind of like ripping off a Band-Aid. I overheard Lilith asking a witch why the spell she put on me so I wouldn't feel the mating pull did not last." Before the words were completely out of my mouth, Tempest hissed, and then she roared.

"She did what? I'll kill her myself! How dare she do this to you both? What the fuck was she thinking? Why can't I kill her? You know I can't kill her, right? Even though I want to. That's not how Hell works. But I am Satan. Why can't I do what I want?" She finally took a break from yelling. If she kept it up, she would have a sore throat by the end of this conversation.

"Tempest, I get it. I want to kill her, too. She kept me from my mate for two years. But we can't do that. We're both better than that, and you're right; that's not the way Hell works. Yes, you are Satan, and you run the joint. So, could you make a decision that breaks the laws of Hell? Sure! But that's not you, and you know it. There must be another way to handle this."

Abaddon was right. Killing my mother was not the answer. Although, at this point, I could do it with my own bare hands and not care. "Abaddon is right, Tempest. You can't do that. None of us can. I would vote for that law to change in case anything similar happens in the future. She needs to be punished, though, and harshly. I'll never forgive her for this."

Tempest sat there for a few minutes, deep in thought. "I think there's only one thing to do. I'm going to travel up to Heaven and have a talk with my brother. This is too much, and he needs to help me figure out a way to punish her. This isn't a good time for a trip, but it will be a quick trip. Being in Heaven makes me itch. Why don't you two go up to your suite, Abby, and we'll talk more before I leave in the morning? Tonight, I think you two should relax and spend some time together."

I looked at Abaddon, and he looked at me. I heard him say in my head that he couldn't think of a better idea. We both got up from the couch. Abaddon picked me up in his arms, and we said our goodbyes. This could wait until tomorrow. Tonight, all I wanted was to be in my Demon's arms.

CHAPTER NINETEEN

tempest visits heaven

JACOB and I were in our bedroom, getting ready to go visit Bob in Heaven. He hated it when I called him by his given name. He could be such a pompous ass sometimes. Yes, he was God, but he was also Bob, and I was his sister, damn it! I should be able to call my brother by his name. Sometimes, I did it just to annoy him. What else was a baby sister for?

"So, baby, how do you feel about meeting Bob?"

My mate chuckled. He was the only person I'd ever talked to about my complicated relationship with my brother, so he understood I was just being a brat when I called my brother Bob.

"You mean, how do I feel about meeting God? Let's just say I'm more afraid of meeting him than I was of meeting you."

I threw the hairbrush in my hand at him, narrowly missing his head. I could have hit him if I wanted to. However, I would never do that. I loved that man more than I loved my Demon life. "Seriously? You're more afraid of meeting the original do-gooder than you were of meeting the leader of Hell?"

He caught my brush and walked over to me, grabbing me by my waist and kissing me hard. I could stay here kissing him all day. But if we don't stop, we won't be getting up to Heaven today. "Baby, meeting you didn't scare me as much because I accepted long ago that I'd end up down here and not up there. So, I had plenty of time to get used to the idea of meeting you. In my wildest dreams, I never thought I'd meet your brother."

His explanation made sense, but I wasn't sure I believed it. I was happy he was never afraid of me, even before we met. I hated the idea of Jacob ever being afraid of me.

I couldn't help but wonder what made him think he would end up in Hell. Most people who ended up here were shocked, even the ones who had committed the most heinous crimes. Although I hadn't known him long, there didn't seem to be anything that would make him think he'd end up down here. "You always thought you'd end up in Hell? Would you like to share what you've done to come to that conclusion" I teased him.

"If I tell you, I'd have to kill you. Seriously, nothing major. Mostly stuff when I was a kid. Some shoplifting, drinking when I was about 15, and I dabbled in drugs when I was in my early twenties. Smoked pot and ate an occasional edible. I was mostly joking when I said that, although I've never been 100% sure I would get into Heaven."

"Okay, my nephew is going to be at my brother's castle in about a half hour to see me and meet you. I know he doesn't want to be alone with his father for that long, so we should head out soon. Are you all packed?"

"I'm packed and ready to go. I still can't believe that Jesus has issues with his father. Who would have guessed that?"

I smiled as I thought of my nephew. As much as my brother drove me crazy, my nephew brought me undeniable joy from the day he was born. I loved it when he came down to Hell to visit me and some friends he had down here. What I'd never tell my brother was he preferred being in Hell. He would miss his mother if he moved down here; otherwise, he would have done so years ago.

"You know how families can be. My brother can be difficult, too, which doesn't help. He wants to control Jesus, and he can't be, won't be, controlled. If my brother had his way, my nephew would be married with about 100 kids. But Jesus enjoys being single and has no desire to be a dad. He won't give up on it, so Jesus stays away most of the time. Anyway, can you carry the luggage, or do you want me to get someone to help?"

He grabbed the bags by the door. "I've got it. Let's head down to the portal. The quicker we leave, the quicker we get back. I know Heaven makes you itch," he said, smirking at me.

It didn't take us long to arrive outside my brother's mansion. "You were right. Traveling by portals does get easier every time," Jacob said as he looked around, eyes wide. Not only was it a sight to behold, but most humans didn't get to see it until death.

"This is beautiful, Tempest. Is that your brother's home? And where are the clouds? I pictured Heaven as clouds floating around, with everything on top of them, and angels walking around in long white robes, halos, and large wings. There's plenty of angels walking around, but they're all dressed in regular clothes."

His idea of Heaven made me laugh because it sounded like what I always imagined humans thought of it. "Jacob, how would everyone live if everything was on clouds? Walking on clouds would be impossible. Everyone would fall through to Earth. In a lot of ways, Heaven and Hell are similar to Earth. Although Heaven doesn't have all of the pollution Earth has. The beaches are beautiful up here, too."

He was staring at my brother's house now in awe. I couldn't blame him. There probably wasn't a more beautiful home in any realm. It covered what would be about four football fields. It was all one house, not a main house with smaller houses around it.

The color was off-white and had intricate details, such as stately columns that framed the many doors. To add a touch of color, the window shutters were all cobalt blue. As you approached the mansion, a grand staircase led to the main front door. The landscaping around the property was meticulously designed, with vibrant flowers and well-trimmed shrubs enhancing the overall aesthetic.

As we were standing there, I saw my brother approach us. That was new. He never met guests at the portal, not even his only sister. "Hey, Bob. How ya doing?" He gave me the evil glare that he had perfected over the years.

"It's God, Tempest, you know that."

I'd missed him so much. I'd never admit it to anyone but Jacob, but I'd truly missed him. We began repairing our relationship years ago but still didn't see each other often enough.

He stopped glaring at me and grabbed me in a tight hug. "I've missed you, my sister. You need to visit more often." I hugged him back just as tightly.

"I've missed you too, Bob. When you visit Hell at least once, I'll visit Heaven more." He let me go and shook Jacob's hand.

"Jacob, it's nice to meet you. You have your hands full with this one, you know that, right? If you ever need a break from my sister, come over to visit. You're always welcome."

"Why would he need a break from me? I'm perfectly charming. Unlike you, Bob. You are always so surly. It's good to laugh occasionally."

He laughed. "I truly have missed you, Tempest. I'm glad you're here, even though judging by your cryptic call to me, the reason you're here isn't good."

That made me growl. "Unfortunately, it's not, Bob. Let's head to your castle, and I'll explain it all."

Bob

I had missed my sister. No one else could get away with calling me by my given name. Pretending it annoyed me was fun, but hearing her say it brought back so many wonderful memories of our childhood. When Tempest was born, I was already ten years old. I loved her so much until she turned five, and she always wanted to be around me and my friends. What 15-year-old boy wants his baby sister hanging around all the time?

Then, when she was 20 and I was 25, things started changing in Heaven. Suddenly, crime began to happen more often, and we were fast becoming a lawless society. Someone needed to take control, and I did just that. It had been so long that I didn't remember where the title God came from, but it took off.

A lot was still being created back then. Earth and humans were still a long way off, as was Hell. None of us ever imagined what the world would become, but I don't think anyone ever does. I was sure humans in the 50s never imagined the changes that would be made in the future.

Tempest hated it when I began running Heaven. I had a lot of responsibility and less time for my baby sister. Then, when Jesus was born, I had even more responsibility. We slowly stopped spending time together, and she seemed to become bitter about it all. That's when she jumped from Heaven. She liked to tell people I pushed her, but I never figured out why, other than to make me look bad.

When she jumped, I was worried about her. We didn't know a lot about what was outside of Heaven. Would she be able to survive? Not only did she survive, but she thrived. She and the other original Demons built Hell basically from the ground up. They'd kept it up to date to this day. Every time things changed in the "normal world," Tempest also ensured those changes happened in Hell.

I was so proud of her. She had worked her ass off. She was also a very fair and kind leader. If I was being honest with myself, she was fairer than me. I usually have high expectations of the Angels in Heaven, while Tempest was more of a "let them live their lives" kind of leader.

I didn't realize how deep in thought I was until we reached my office. We all got comfortable on the lounge chairs in my office, and Tempest began her story. "Bob, Lilith has gone too far this time, and I don't know how to handle the situation. She needs to be punished, but she needs a punishment more severe than my usual type of reprimand. You know I've never been able to come up with suitable punishments."

I had to laugh at that. Tempest had never been good at punishments. She was a teacher before she jumped from Heaven, and some of our younger Angels could be quite challenging. Her boss used to have to talk to her about her punishments all the time.

Suddenly, I heard Tempest calling my name. I got lost in my memories again. "Sorry, Tempest, go on. You have my full attention."

"Abaddon is Lilac's mate..."

I interrupted her before she could finish her sentence. "Isn't Lilac Lilith's youngest daughter? Oh, she must hate that." My sister grew visibly angry. This wasn't good. Could I sneak out without hearing the issue? Probably not.

"No, she didn't like it. Abaddon has known for two years, since Lilac turned 18, that she was his mate. However, Lilac never felt the mate pull." That was odd. Mates always felt the mate pull unless they were human. Then they might not.

"How did she not know Abaddon was her mate? That's not even possible."

"You're right; it's not. Abaddon and I have discussed it over the last two years and thought maybe it was possible, but we never realized it. Yesterday, Lilac and Abaddon went to Purgatory to visit Lilith and give her the good news. Lilith didn't agree. She went to her office to make a call, and Lilac followed her. She heard Lilith speaking to someone on the phone. Lilith asked the person on the other side of the phone why the spell she put on Lilac to suppress the mating pull didn't last."

My sister was right. Lilith had gone too far this time. "Tempest, I can't help but wonder why you came to me with this. I will help you with this problem, don't get me wrong. I'm curious why you came to me because you must know my answer, and you won't like it."

Tempest looked down at her hands, but before she did, I could see the tears forming in her eyes. "I know, Bob. That's why I came here. I knew you would be the only one to tell me the truth about this."

I felt bad for my sister. This would not be easy on her. She didn't find it easy to take another life.

"Tempest, we have no choice but to kill her. You convinced me to put her in Purgatory, hoping she would change there. However, it seems like she has gotten worse. If she would do that to Lilac, whom she loves beyond measure, we can't trust her not to hurt or possibly kill someone. Perhaps even Abaddon, to get him away from her daughter. I know what you think about me, but trust me, I hate this. She's one of my oldest friends, too."

I knew my brother was right. There was a time when we were all the best of friends. That was before Lilith started on her crime spree in Hell. Lilith always thought she was better than anyone else and could get away with anything. It started when she was a child because her parents spoiled her rotten.

But it had never been that bad until she met Bill. Until that point, it had been small things like taking what she wanted instead of asking for it or paying for it. But when she met Bill, things changed. It was as if they brought out the worst in each other. We were all surprised when they robbed the bank and killed the guards. At that point, we were done with her.

Jacob took Tempest in his arms as she sobbed uncontrollably. He held her until she got it all out. I was glad my sister found him. He was a good man who treated her like a Goddess.

"I know you're right, Bob. We can't allow her to live. One reason I came here is to get the sword of life. It's the only thing that will kill any Demon our age."

I wouldn't let her do this. She might be Satan, but she would never recover from this. "I won't let you do this, Tempest."

She looked at me, confused. "What do you mean? You just said we must do this." I looked my sister in the eyes before responding.

"You will not do it, Tempest; I will. I helped set this in motion all those years ago. I must be the one to put a stop to the madness."

CHAPTER TWENTY

christmas in hell!

THE RE HAD BEEN SO MUCH GOING on in Hell that I forgot the day the humans celebrated my brother's birthday was fast approaching. It might seem strange that Satan or Hell cared that it was Christmas. But first, God was my brother. It was true that we didn't always get along, but we loved each other.

Technically, it wasn't my brother's birthday, but since it was when humans celebrated it, that was when Heaven and Hell celebrated it. Honestly, those of us who were original Angels and Demons didn't remember when our birthdays were. When you were as old as we are, it stopped being important.

But Christmas was usually as big a day in Heaven and Hell as on Earth. No one knew this, but I'd been hoping my brother would come down to Hell to celebrate his birthday for one year. I went up to Heaven about 10 years ago and always gave him a gift.

Since I'd been in the castle working so much lately, it was easy to forget the time of the year. Everyone in Hell made a big deal at Christmas time. However, no one ever started decorating the castle until I gave the word. I totally forgot, which meant I didn't give the word to decorate.

Jacob and I were going to go back to Hell before we went to Purgatory with Bob. Bob needed to get out the sword of life and had some other preparations to make. This gave Jacob and me time to spend some quality time together. We were still solving some issues in Hell, but I needed a break right now.

I also needed to spend some alone time with my mate. When Jacob and I were ready to leave, Jacob and Bob started acting weird. They both had big, stupid grins on their faces. And when they thought I wasn't paying attention, they gave each other secretive looks.

I let it go until we got to the portal, but once we were there, I couldn't help but ask what was going on. "Spill it, Jacob. What are you and my brother up to? You both were acting suspiciously back there."

He just looked at me with that stupid grin. "I do not know what you're talking about, baby. Your brother and I aren't up to anything. I was just trying to be nice because I know this isn't easy on either of you."

He was lying through his ridiculously white teeth; I knew that. Even if his face didn't show it, I could feel it in our bond. I let it go again. I knew that neither Jacob nor my brother would try to hurt me. Jacob was my mate, so he couldn't if he wanted to, and I knew that no matter what difficulties my brother and I had, he would never hurt me either. Jacob would tell me when he was ready; no need to push him.

Once we got out of the portal, I saw it was snowing in Hell. I know that might sound weird because of the way humans thought about Hell, but we had four seasons, although our winters were usually mild, and it rarely snowed. It was pretty. I'd always wished it snowed more down here. I looked towards the castle and noticed what Jacob was up to. "Jacob," I said with tears forming in my eyes.

Christmas lights lit up the castle, and someone decorated the tree in front of the castle for Christmas. I jumped into his arms, wanting to feel him holding me. "How did you do this so quickly? We weren't in Heaven that long. And how did I forget it was Christmas? This is beautiful, darling. Thank you."

He was looking down at me, love shining through his eyes. "Do you ever remember how many people we have working and living in the castle? I realized you hadn't mentioned Christmas, so I figured you forgot about it with everything that was going on. Abaddon and I had a talk with every supervisor in the castle and let them know we wanted them to prepare for Christmas while we were gone as a surprise to you. Everyone adores you, so no one had any complaints."

I started mentally trying to figure out the date. "Oh my God, Christmas is tomorrow!" Jacob gently put me down to grab what little we brought with us.

"It is my love. Everything should be ready. The cooks even went through past Christmas dinner menus to pick the perfect dinner. Merry Christmas, baby." Now, I started sobbing right outside my castle. Not a very Satan-like thing to do.

"Thank you so much, love. This is the best Christmas ever, and it's all because of you. Now let's go so I can see the decorations!" I always felt like a little kid at this time of the year. It truly is my favorite holiday. It always reminded me of my and my brother's birthdays back when we were kids. He grabbed the two bags in one hand and one of my hands in his other.

I was amazed when we walked into the castle. The staff had truly outdone themselves this time. Everyone who worked in the castle, in any position, would get a large Christmas bonus. I would have to talk to Abaddon to see if we could have it deposited into everyone's accounts tomorrow. I didn't think it would be possible, so it would probably be a little late. We'd add a couple hundred dollars to compensate for being late.

In the center of the room stood an enormous Christmas tree, reaching toward the ceiling. The decorations were a mix of traditional ornaments, sparkling lights, and delicate tinsel. Beneath the tree sat carefully wrapped presents in festive paper and bows that added to the anticipation of the holiday celebrations.

The fireplace mantel was adorned with garlands of fresh pine. A crackling fire added warmth to the room, creating a cozy ambiance, even in the large room. Stockings hung from the mantel, with a stocking with my name and one that said Jacob in the middle of the other stockings.

It seemed like every corner of the castle was touched by the spirit of Christmas. Everyone had truly gone above and beyond while we were in Heaven visiting my brother.

"There is one more surprise, Tempest." I couldn't imagine what else there could be, but before I could ask, the doorbell rang. "Why don't you get that, baby? We're right here, so we shouldn't disturb the staff."

Well, that was odd. Normally, he'd been answering the door since moving in. I walked to the door, not knowing what to expect.

What, or I should say who, I saw standing there started me sobbing again. It was my brother. I threw myself at him. He had two bags with him, so it looked like he was staying for at least a few days. I was going to spend Christmas with my brother! I broke away from him and turned back to my mate. "You did this, didn't you?" He came over, shook my brother's hand, and put his arm around me.

"God and I talked. I remember you telling me about Christmas in Hell and how you've wanted your brother to visit you at Christmas time for years. We talked about everything that has been happening and how it seemed like you had forgotten Christmas this year. I told him you have been waiting for him to visit for Christmas for years. Your brother loves you as much as you love him. He agreed right away to spend Christmas in Hell with us."

"Jacob is right, Tempest. I know we've had problems over the years, but you're still my sister. I'll love you forever. And for us, forever is a very long time."

That last part made me chuckle. Forever truly was a very long time for us. Without the sword of death, neither of us was going anywhere. And we were the only two able to even touch it. We would never kill each other.

While we were talking, a staff member came up to us. He bowed to me and God and asked if he could take God's bags. Once we were standing there, alone again, Jacob was the first to speak up as he put an arm around each of our shoulders. "Well, you two, there should be a cocktail party in the ballroom right now, with a 5-course meal served in the formal kitchen afterward. How about we head over to the ballroom?"

He didn't have to ask either of us twice.

When we walked into the ballroom, all the conversation stopped. I didn't think anyone knew what to do with God in the castle. The whole thing made me giggle. "Yes, everyone, my brother is here. He's going to be here for the next couple of days to celebrate Christmas with us. I ask you to treat him with the same respect you treat me. After all, he's my brother, but he's also God."

We all walked further into the ballroom, shaking hands and saying hi to everyone. I had my mate and my brother here in my castle for Christmas. I didn't stop smiling all night. We still had a lot to deal with, but it could all wait until after Christmas.

CHAPTER TWENTY-ONE
lilac learns lilith's fate

ONE REASON GOD came down to Hell to visit Christmas Eve was to talk to Lilic about her mother's punishment for what she did by binding Lilac's powers so she wouldn't recognize me as her mate. Bob was in Hell longer than he planned. He was only going to stay a few days to a week, and it's now been almost two weeks. He and Tempest were going to Purgatory tomorrow, and then he'd be going back home to Heaven. It was time to let Lilac know what her mother's punishment was. No one wanted her to find out from someone else.

By the time we all jumped from Heaven, we were between 200 to 350 years old. Tempest and I were the oldest, both of us being 350 years old. When Tempest jumped, Lilith and I followed soon after. Tempest was, and always had been, the ruler of Hell, but Lilith, me, and a bunch of other original Demons built Hell with her. Of course, we've had Demons come along who have added to Hell, but it was us who built it in the beginning.

This was one reason I had a hard time swallowing Lilith's fate. This wasn't something that we hadn't talked about before. Lilith had been on her plan for years, and she did whatever the Hell she wanted to. No matter whom she hurt. That was probably why learning what she did to Lilac and I shouldn't have surprised me. She never cared whom she hurt, even if she had given birth to them.

Lilith had 153 daughters and had hurt many of them. Lilac had always been different. Until Fate and Destiny paired her with me. It turned out that Lilith hated me because she thought I helped make the decision to send her to Purgatory. The last person she wanted Lilac with was me. That was probably not true. The last person she wanted Lilac with was mostly likely Bob. As if God would be with a Demon.

Lilac should have been on her way to the castle, where I still lived. I would be moving into Lilac's house in two weeks. I couldn't wait to live with her, but some things had to be done at the castle first, such as capturing the opposition, getting Gusion out of jail, and reuniting with Kali. We wanted Lilac to stay here in case the opposition went after her. She refused, so we set her up with 24-hour guards.

As if she knew I was thinking about her, she appeared at my door. I heard her ask me to open up for her through our mate link. Curious why she wasn't using the key I had given her, I opened the door. I couldn't even see my beautiful mate underneath the pile of boxes that she was holding. I grabbed the boxes from her. "Whoa, beautiful. What's going on here?"

Her smile made my heart swell. She was up to something. "You're moving in with me in two weeks. I think it's about time we started packing. There's no reason we can't start moving some of your stuff over to our place." I swore I'd never tire of hearing her call her house our place

Tonight, I was going to ask her to stay here for the night. I knew she was furious with her mother, but hearing that Lilith was going to be killed was bound to hurt, whether she admitted it or not. There were Demons out there who wouldn't care much, but Lilac was not

SATAN, IS THAT YOU?

one of those Demons. I put the boxes down in a corner and turned to kiss her and hold her tight. It was all I could do not to carry her back to my bedroom.

She jumped and wrapped her legs around my waist, deepening the kiss. Tempest, Jacob, and Bob were expecting us soon, so I had to pull away. "As much as I'd rather finish this in the bedroom with you writhing under me, we have to head down to Tempest's office soon. I wanted to ask if you'd like to spend the night here with me." I smirked at her before continuing. "We can even start packing my stuff up."

She smacked my ass hard. "If I'm spending the night, we will not be packing. Trust me. Do you know why Tempest wants to speak to me? The curiosity is getting to me."

I wouldn't lie to her, but I also couldn't tell her what Tempest and Bob wanted to discuss with her. "Yes, I know, darling. I wish I could tell you, but Tempest and Bob want to be the ones to tell you."

"Okay, then let's head down. We're not that early. I'm sure this has something to do with my mother's punishment, and I want to get it over with."

I grabbed my keys off the coffee table, and we headed out the door. She was tense, but there was no way I could help her until she knew what was going on. Once she was told, I could help her in any way she needed. It's all going to depend on how she takes the news. I just hoped she didn't feel like she had to hide what she felt. If she was upset, that would be understandable.

As we neared the office, we noticed the door was open. We heard Tempest yell to come in before we even reached the door. "Hi, you two. I'm glad you could join us today."

I snickered. "When you're summoned not only by Satan but by God too, what choice do you have but to show up?"

Tempest laughed at my comment. "You're probably right there. Few beings would dare to refuse a summons from my brother and me. Have a seat; get comfortable."

Once we were all seated, Tempest deferred to her brother by pointedly looking at him. "You've always wanted me to be the bearer of bad news, Temp. But yes, I think it's a good idea for me to begin this. Lilac, not only is Lilith your mother, but she's also a big part of the history of both Heaven and Hell. Big enough for her to be in the history books on both planes. Because of that, there is nothing about your mother's history that you don't know."

Bob stopped for a minute, giving Lilac a chance to speak. "We've made a decision that was difficult for all of us. As you know, your mom, Tempest, Abaddon, and I all grew up together. We were all very close during those years. The problem is your mom won't learn from her mistakes. She's been given so many chances but always screws up. It's for that reason that we've made the hard decision that she has to die."

I heard Lilac gasp, and I reached out for her, but she pulled back. "I'm okay, Abby. This isn't a surprise for me. Like God said, I know everything my mom has done, and she refuses to stop. No matter how many chances she has been given. Hearing the words just shook me a little. Can I ask a favor?"

Satan and God nodded their heads.

"Can I please see my mom before it happens? I hate what she did to Abaddon and me, and I agree this is the only option. The thing is, she's still my mom. Saying goodbye will be hard, but I need to do it. Few people will care, not even my sisters, so I want her to know I still love her no matter what."

"I can't speak for God, but that's okay with me. You'll have a guard with you because we can't trust her anymore. However, the guard will give you as much privacy as possible. Also, Abaddon, you will not be her guard."

I immediately tensed up. I wanted to fight her on this. However, I knew I wouldn't win. Especially since God would be on her side with this. "Yes, my liege."

She looked at me, surprised, before she continued. "I want to get this done as soon as possible. I don't think waiting will help any of us. Plus, Bob needs to get back up to Heaven. We don't want the Angels getting out of control while their leader is gone. We'll be leaving for Purgatory at noon tomorrow. Get some rest, everyone. Tomorrow will not be easy on any of us."

CHAPTER TWENTY-TWO

gusion and kali reunite

BLADE and I were in charge of the mission to take down Bastien, but we had the best guards from Hell with us. There was no way this was going to end in any other way than us taking him in. There had been too many attempts to take down Tempest, which would end today. But before that happened, we had to rescue Kali. This would be the easy part, we hoped.

It took our top investigators to find where she was being held. She had been at her mother's the entire time. Her mother, Justine, had no choice but to tell Gusion that Kali had been taken. Kali was in another room with the guard. He had told her he would slit Kali's throat if he heard one wrong word. Justine knew there would be enough time for him to do that before Gusion got to the room to save Kali.

I went to the house alone. We knew everyone in Bastien's army was there due to blackmail, so we had no doubt it would be easy to convince him to walk away. He didn't hear me sneak up on him. "Lucien, you need to let me in there. We know what's been happening, and we're going to take down Bastien tonight. I need to know Kali is safe before we do that."

He spun around, and I saw the hope in his eyes. "It's over, Lucien, or it will be soon. I promise you. Will you make this easy on us both and let me get Kali?" He nodded his head and opened the door for me. Another Demon from Tempest's army walked up behind him.

"He's right, Lucien. It will all be over tonight. I need you to come back to the castle with me, but it's not to take you in."

Lucien handed his weapon over as I walked into the house to let Kali know she was safe. She and Justine sat in the living room, staring at the door. They must have heard our conversation through the door.

"Kali, are you ready to see Gusion?"

She quietly said yes, tears falling down her face. The other guard with me came in to take her to her mate.

Now, it was time to take down Bastien.

As we finally entered their domain, we saw Bastien in the center of his army. While the other men looked nervous, he looked like he was sure he would win this. "Demons, we've talked to others who have escaped and Demons we've captured. We know you don't want to be here. Bastien has blackmailed each of you. If you put down your weapons, you'll be welcomed back. If you don't, you may lose your lives tonight."

They slowly began dropping their weapons until Bastien was the only one left holding one. "I would think about this before giving in. I'll get away, and you will all pay. Remember what I used to blackmail you. If you do, you'll pick up your weapons and join me in this fight."

Not one of them picked up their weapons. They knew as well as we did that this would end tonight. That included whatever it was that Bastien held over each of their heads. While we stood there talking, Blade snuck in from his place on the side. Out of the corner of my

JANET LEE SMITH

eye, I saw him creeping behind Bastien. I only needed to keep him talking long enough for Blade to get behind him and take him down.

Many people would have seen Blade coming, even though he was very careful in his moves. But Bastien was so full of himself and sure we wouldn't take him that he was only paying attention to me. By the time he realized Balde was behind him, he had a blade to his neck and couldn't move without being stabbed.

The rest was easy. His army came with us willingly, and Blade stayed behind him, holding the blade to his throat with one hand while not holding Bastien's hands behind his back with the other. He struggled at first, but before long, he knew he would not get away.

Each Demon in his army was welcomed back into Tempest's army after talking to one of Hell's top psychologists. Tempest gave them each a month's vacation to adjust to life after what they'd been through and to spend some time with their loved ones.

Gusion...

It had been two weeks since Ruby opened my cell door, and I walked out of the dungeon. My life was just getting back to normal. Satan's army had found Kali right before they took down the opposition leader. They brought her to me in the dungeons right away. I thought I was seeing an Angel. I had tried to hope we would be together again, but my hope had dwindled that week.

Since no one could see into the dungeons except those down here, my cell bars were never locked. They had made me as comfortable as possible. I heard two people walking down the hallway. I knew one was Ruby. I recognized the sound of her walking. The other person, I wasn't so sure. As they got closer, I knew who it was. I'd know that scent anywhere. That was my mate. I ran out of my cell and the short distance between me and Kali.

Briefly, I noticed Ruby turn around the other way and walk away. I quickly caught up to Kali and picked her up in my arms, swinging her around. She jumped up, wrapping her legs around my waist. I started kissing her like I was a drowning man, and she held all the

120

water in the world. As soon as my mouth met hers, I ran my tongue over the seam, demanding entrance.

My hands roamed all over her body as I carried her into my cell. I walked over to the bed and gently threw her on top of it while she giggled. I kneeled on top of her and removed her clothes, kissing and sucking her neck while I did so. Suddenly, I heard someone clearing their throat behind us, and I growled. Kali giggled again while pulling her clothes back on.

Before I turned around, I heard Ruby come into my cell. "Is this our high school reunion, and I forgot the day?" I asked the two women behind me as I turned around, trying to keep my anger in check.

"I tried to stop her, Gusion, but she is Satan. She kind of runs the place."

"You didn't try very hard, now did you, Ruby?"

I knew none of us could stop Tempest from doing anything she wanted to do. After all, she was Hell's ruler. No matter how fair she was, Hell was still her domain. She also has a bratty streak, so knowing that Kali and I were down here after our separation would be hard for her to stay away from. She thought she was funny. I was not finding her amusing right now. "Tempest, what the actual fuck are you doing here right now?"

I heard Kali's quick intake of breath. She wasn't used to people talking to Satan that way. Satan and I grew up together, but even if we hadn't, Tempest didn't like people to kiss her ass. While we original Demons get away with a lot with Tempest, we also know where the line is, and we know better than to cross that line. Tempest knew what she was doing here and what my reaction would be. Knowing Tempest, I would have disappointed her if I had reacted in any other way.

Tempest looked back at Kali and responded to her and not me. "Kali, it's okay. Gusion and I are old, old friends. He has a valid question, I guess." She looked back at me. "Gusion, did you really think I would miss this moment? I didn't think you would try to rip her clothes off already, though."

"Did you think at all, Tempest? Of course, I would try to rip my mate's clothes off already! We've been separated for months! I know you, Tempest. You knew exactly what would go on down here. You figured it would be fun to interrupt us." I looked back, and Ruby was smirking. "Look at Ruby. She knew what you were doing, too. You're one of my oldest friends, Tempest, and I love you. I feel I must tell you that if that weren't the case, I'd be strangling you right now."

Tempest's trilling laugh filled my cell. "I'd like to see you try, Demon. We both know how that would end."

Ruby was still near my cell door but clearly couldn't help putting her two cents in. "We can guess what would happen with your punishments, Tempest. Gusion would be topside in a little, fluffy white kitten body, being the familiar to a terrible witch. Forced to help her with her magic."

Tempest didn't even try to deny it. Even Kali laughed at that because everyone in Hell knew Satan's punishments. "Okay, you two. You can either both leave my cell or stand there and watch me while I ravish my mate. Your choice. But either way, I'm about to fuck my mate, and when we're done, we'll slow it down so I can make love to her."

Kali started laughing as Tempest and Ruby both ran out of the cell. Knowing my friends as I do, I knew that would work. I wouldn't have done it, but I knew that just the thought of it would make them leave. I leaned over my mate again, kissing her while undoing the clothes that I had already undone once. There might not be a wall or door to hide what we were doing, but I was sure Tempest would not return. And there was no one else that Ruby couldn't stop from coming down that hall. The rest of the night was about Kali and me. I would leave her with no question about how much I love her.

This night was the beginning of the rest of our lives, and I was determined to make the most of it.

CHAPTER TWENTY-THREE
abaddon and lilac

WHILE TEMPEST and Bob would not allow Lilac to be present when they confronted Lilith and ended her, they did agree with me being there. When we arrived in Purgatory, we went straight to Lilith's house. When she opened the door and saw the three of us together, a look of fear crossed across her face. It was fleeting, but it was there.

"Well, well, well, what brings you three here? What could I have possibly done that would have Satan and God at my door? And together at that. Her tone was cocky, but she hesitated at the end. She knew this wasn't good. She couldn't see the sword of life because God and Satan both had the power to conceal it.

Bob spoke since it was decided that he would handle this situation. "You know what you've done, Lilith. Keeping Abadoon's mate from him would have driven him crazy at some point. Heck, it was possible that Lilac would have gone crazy, too, since we don't know how the spell would ultimately affect her. You know how when you killed those two guards. Now I get my wish. You die today, Lilith."

Before she had a chance to say anything or react at all, God plunged the sword of life into her chest. The moment it went through her heart, she disintegrated into ashes. As Tempest broke down in tears, I took her in my arms to comfort her. This was hard on us all, but it had to be done.

The leader of Purgatory had been informed this was happening today, so he would handle everything from here. Once Tempest had calmed down a little, we headed back to the portal, none of us saying a word.

It had been a little over a week since Satan, God, and I went to Purgatory to "handle" the problem once known as Lilith. I was glad Tempest and Bob denied Lilac's request to be there. I didn't think she would have ever gotten over that. She was mad at her mom over what she did to us, and she knew her mother would never change. But Lilith was still her mother.

For us original Demons, we left Heaven, our home, under horrible circumstances when we were already hundreds of years old. That did something to a Demon. We were all a little jaded. Finding Lilac helped me a lot with that. I wanted to take her mind off what happened, so I was taking her on vacation topside to visit Cape Cod.

Somehow, Lilac had only been topside a few times, and she had never been to the Cape. I couldn't wait to show her the beauty of the area.

"Hey, baby, whatcha doing in here?" I turned around and noticed her standing in the kitchen doorway.

"Hey honey, I'm getting some of Hell's best champagne to bring with us. The stuff they sell topside is good, but it doesn't compare to Hell's. Is there anything else you want to bring from the kitchen?"

"Not really. It's been a long time since I've been topside, and one of the things I'm most looking forward to is the food. The champagne is a good idea, though. I remember the champagne up there; it is lousy compared to Hell's. You said we're going to Cape Cod, right?"

It took me a minute, but I noticed her hands were behind her back.

"We are. We own a house on the beach in Provincetown. What do you have behind your back, Lilac?"

She blushed. "Well, I was thinking since we're going to the beach, I needed a new bikini." She pulled a neon pink bikini from behind her back. It had very little material to it. I couldn't help but growl—both in lust and consternation.

I slowly stalked over to her and took her in my arms. I whispered in her ear, "Baby, I can't wait to see you in that. However, can you please only wear it on our beach? I'd hate to rip out the eyes of any humans."

She giggled like she didn't quite believe me.

"Baby, I'm serious. If I see anyone looking at you when you're wearing that, I won't be responsible for what I do. I can't wait to see you in it, but no one else better see you in it."

She kept giggling, but I could see something feral in her eyes. "Okay, you win. But only because if anyone watched you while you were wearing something so small, it wouldn't be pretty. Even if it was some big dude who was human, I'd tear him apart."

"Let's set that boundary right now, then. Whenever we wear only a little of clothing, we will be only around each other."

Her smile lit up her entire face. "That works for me! Will there be any way for anyone to see us on the beach at your house? Because I have a speedo for you to wear while we're on the Cape."

I didn't even know where to begin with that. A speedo? Oh, Satan.

"First, beautiful, it's not my house; it's our house. We've been over this. Anything that is mine is yours, too. Second, no one will see us. I have high fences all around the beach area. And...a speedo? Are you serious right now?"

She reached into her pocket and pulled out a neon pink Speedo that matched her bikini perfectly. "Please? You'll look so hot in it!"

"Really, Lilac? Not only a Speedo but a neon pink one? You know what would happen if any other Demons saw me in that, right? You're so lucky that I love you. Go put it in the suitcase. I think other than your bikini and that abomination, we're ready to go. My house-keeper should have everything ready for us by now. I'm so glad some Demons lived topside. I would hate to have to explain some things to a human housekeeper."

She gave me a quick peck on my cheek before running from the room to put the bathing suits in a bag near the door. "I'm almost ready. I'll meet you at the door in five minutes," she said as she was leaving. Grabbing the champagne, I put it in the backpack I had with me in the kitchen.

Looking around, I realized I had made the right decision to move into her house. I still had my rooms at the castle. Tempest liked all her top generals to have a suite there in case of emergency. But this was our home. The home I shared with my mate. I'd never been so content in my eternal life. I sighed, walked over to the door, and saw Lilac waiting for me.

The house wasn't as grand as the castle, of course. No house was except for God's mansion. It sat on a corner lot and had a well-main-tained yard. The grass was always cut, and shrubs lined the yard instead of a fence. A rose bush with beautiful pink roses was on either side of the front door. My favorite part was the swing set in the backyard. Lilac had told me she had that put in because she knew she wanted children one day. I couldn't wait to watch our kids playing on that swing one day.

The inside was beautiful. While she could have had an interior designer decorate the house, she decided to do it herself. The living room had large floor-to-ceiling windows. It was painted beige, and the light coming in from the windows brightened the room.

The kitchen was Lilac's favorite room because she loved to cook. Granite countertops spanned the room, offering plenty of room for food preparation. Underneath, spacious cabinets with glass-fronted doors provided ample storage for cookware, utensils, and pantry essentials.

A large island was in the center of the room, serving as both a workspace and a gathering spot for family and friends. The island had a built-in sink, which made meal preparation and clean-up a breeze.

The appliances were all stainless steel. A state-of-the-art refrigerator, complete with a water and ice dispenser, stood beside a sleek oven with a gas cooktop. There was a range hood above that removed lingering cooking odors.

Realizing Lilac was going to meet me at the door, I hurried over and found her already standing there. I took her in my arms, feeling her melt against me. I kissed her with all the love and passion that I had in me. We were still kissing when I scented her arousal. It was time to get out of here, or we would never leave.

"Let's go, baby," I said, grabbing the bags. We walked to the portal because we didn't want to leave either of our cars at the castle for the week we'd be gone.

Tempest had allowed me to have a portal in the backyard at my house on the Cape, right outside my deck and just feet from the beach. I blindfolded Lilac before we got to our destination. I couldn't wait to see her face when she saw the beauty of Cape Cod. As soon as the portal door opened, the Demon taking care of the property was outside to grab our bags. "Hey, Jose. Thank you so much. Would you take our things up to the master bedroom?"

He nodded his head yes as he looked quizzically at Lilac with the blindfold. "My mate has never been to the Cape before. I wanted her to wait to see until I had her in the perfect spot."

Jose smiled. I knew he understood because it was a similar situation when he met his mate. I looked out over the sand toward the water. It always took my breath away.

I grabbed one of Lilac's hands and gently pulled her to the door of the portal. I guided her to the middle of the sand and slowly took the blindfold off her. She gasped and put her hand over her mouth. "It's beautiful, Abby. Look at that sun and the water. Gorgeous."

Suddenly, she took her shoes off and ran towards the water's edge. She bounded into the water, the edges of her dress falling into it. She didn't know what gorgeous was. Gorgeous was her in that water, the sunlight shining down on her. It was at that moment I saw the Angel part of her. Lilith may have been a Demon, but she was one of the original Angels, as we all were. That meant that all her children had a bit of Angel in them. Just like our kids would.

I walked slowly over to her, kicking my shoes off as I went. Once I was over to her, I picked her up and swung her around in my arms. "Every day, I grow to love you more, Lilac. I will spend every day of my life doing everything I can to make you happy. Will you marry me?" I reached into my pocket and pulled out the ring box. "This isn't exactly how I planned this, but seeing you like this, I couldn't stop myself."

Tears were running down her cheeks. "Yes, yes, yes! A thousand times, yes! I don't know how you planned on asking me, but this is perfect. I can't wait to be your wife, Abaddon."

Hugging her tight, I carried her right up the stairs to the bedroom, passing Jose on the way. "Jose, you can leave for the day. You'll still get paid for the time. Go get Suzie and do something special with her."

sharing the news

LILAC AND I have been at our house in the Cape for a week, and it's time to go back to Hell. We enjoyed the time alone together, and if I was being honest, I'd enjoy an extended stay. I planned on talking to Tempest about giving me a month off for our honeymoon. That would be a surprise for Lilac. I knew Tempest wouldn't mind.

We were planning our wedding for Christmas Eve because that would give us six months to plan it. I secretly went up to Heaven when I decided to ask Lilac to marry me so I could ask Bob if we could have the wedding up there, with Bob officiating it. After all, few people, Demons, or angels could say God himself officiated their wedding.

Bob said yes right away. He'd been feeling guilty about the way things ended with Lilith and had been looking for ways to make it up to Lilac. He also believed it would be good for the relationship between Heaven and Hell. For years, there was no relationship. Angels never came down to Hell, and we Demons who still had family up in Heaven rarely went to visit them.

From what I understood, Tempest and Bob had a long talk when he was down in Hell for Christmas last year. Everything that happened with Lilith made them realize we needed to have peace. A lot would have been different with Lilith had the relationship between the two planes of existence been different. Tempest and Bob had a summit planned next month between the two planes here on Earth. They both felt it needed to happen someplace neutral.

I'd deal with that next month. Right now, it was time to wake up my beautiful fiancée. I got up early to make breakfast and was going to serve it to her in bed. When I walked into the bedroom, I saw she had the pillow over her head. She wasn't looking forward to leaving and was trying to avoid it.

I put the breakfast tray on the nightstand by the bed and gently pulled the pillow off her. "Time to wake up, beautiful. I made all your favorites for breakfast." I grabbed a piece of bacon off the tray and placed it close to her nose. She couldn't resist bacon. Hell had a lot of vegetarians, so getting things like bacon could be tough. That was one reason she was looking forward to the food topside. She loved meat.

She growled at me but grabbed the bacon from my hand, quickly devouring it. "Gimme some more," she said, pouting.

"Sit up, and you can have all the bacon. I'll even make you more. I want to have one more swim with you before we leave." That got her interest. She's always enjoyed swimming. Hell had beautiful beaches, but neither of us had been on vacation in a while, so we hadn't been able to enjoy them.

"Okay, you win. I want to take another swim before we leave, too. One more swim before we both go back to work." She pouted again. She was so damn adorable when she pouted.

"We'll come back again for a longer stay as soon as we can, I promise. We'll make more of an effort to go to the beach closest to our home in Hell, too. After all, all work and no play makes Lilac a very boring girl."

She slapped me with the pillow, which is pretty much what I expected her to do. "Come on, let's eat breakfast and go for a swim. I already called Tempest to let her know there's something that we need to talk to her about when we return. One more thing, I accidentally packed our swimsuits, so I guess we'll have to go skinny dipping."

"Accidentally, huh? Why don't I believe that? You just want to see me swim naked."

She wasn't wrong. "If I had my way, you would do everything naked, at least when we're in our own homes." I nibbled on her neck and tickled her stomach while she giggled and tried to get away from me.

We ate our breakfast and went out skinny dipping before ensuring we had packed everything. Once we were sure, I called Jose up in the bedroom to help me with our bags. Somehow, we're leaving with almost double the bags we came with. It couldn't be all the meat that my mate bought to bring home with us. No, it couldn't be that at all.

When we were safely in the portal, I texted Tempest to let her know we were on our way back. She told me she and Jacob were waiting for us in her office. We were going to take the portal to the gardens of Hell, and then we'd get a Huber back to our house. We couldn't wait to give Tempest the good news, so we didn't want to go home first.

When we got out of the portal back in Hell, I noticed two of the staff members from the castle were out there to take our bags for us. "Paul, Tom, it's good to see you both. Can you just bring our bags to the foyer? We came to have a quick conversation with Satan, and then we'll get a Huber home." The Demons nodded and grabbed our bags.

Lilac looked like she was going to be sick. I knew part of the reason was that Tempest had been like a second mother to her since she was born. What Tempest thinks means a lot to her. I grabbed one of her hands in mine as we walked down the hallway to the office. "There's no need to look like you're going to your death, love. Tempest is going to be happy for us."

"I know you're right, honey. She's been so supportive of us. But what if we're wrong? What if she's not happy that we're going to get married?"

I stopped and pulled her to me. "It won't matter, love. We're getting married on Christmas Eve, no matter what. Remember, we're not letting Satan know that we're getting married. We're letting one of my oldest friends know we're getting married."

"Aren't they the same?" she asked me in a timid voice. "Yes, they are the same, but it's going to be okay." I heard a familiar sound behind us. I looked up, and Tempest and Jacob were standing there. "We were wondering what was taking you so long, so we came to look for you."

Jacob laughed at his mate. I had to admit watching someone laugh at Satan would never get old. Especially a human. "What my mate is really saying is she is nosy as Hell and wants to know what's going on. Isn't that right, sweetheart?"

Satan snorted. "I do not know what you're talking about, dear. There's not a nosy bone in my body."

"You're right, beautiful. There's not a nosy bone in your body. There are many nosy bones in your body." I felt Lilac relax in my arms.

"Why don't we go to your office, Tempest? Lilac and I can give you our news."

Lilac looked up at me, smiled, and put her hand on my cheek before kissing me. The wrong hand. She realized what she had done when Tempest started jumping up and down, clapping.

"You're getting married!" Satan squealed. She was worse than a teenage human girl sometimes. She grabbed my mate's hand. "Let me see. Oh, it's beautiful. Good job, Abaddon. You didn't even need my help to pick it out. I'm impressed."

I couldn't help but roll my eyes.

"Who are you rolling your eyes at, Abby? Remember me?" She pointed at herself. "Satan? I run the place?"

Sure, she was Satan, but she was also just jumping up and down like a sorority girl.

"I know who you are, missy, and who are you calling Abby? You know I hate that. Only my fiancée can call me that." It was her turn to roll her eyes at me.

She hugged us both before asking if we wanted a glass of champagne to celebrate. It was only 11:00 am, but she was Satan. Lilac and I were Demons, and we lived in Hell. Who was going to tell us we couldn't have champagne at 11:00 am?

CHAPTER TWENTY-FIVE
satan wants to plan lilac's bridal shower

"JACOB, why are you giving me such a hard time? You know I'd be brilliant at planning Lilac's bridal shower! Plus, with what happened to her mother, I think I should." I watched as Jacob chuckled. Sometimes, he had no respect that I was Satan. I loved him anyway.

"What are you doing, chuckling?" I asked as I zapped his delicious ass. When he jumped, I couldn't help but laugh. He should have expected that.

"Tempest, we've sat here for an hour with you telling me about your ideas for a bridal shower. It's as if you don't know Lilac at all. I even know she would hate it all."

Picking up a pillow, I threw it hard at his head. He just chuckled again. I went over and sat in his lap before continuing. Once I was nice and comfortable and could feel how happy he was to see me, I squirmed a little in his lap while he groaned. "Tempest, you keep that up, and I'm just going to carry you to the bedroom."

"Jacob, I have a wedding shower to plan! No time for your sex shenanigans!!"

He roughly grabbed my wrists and put them behind my back while kissing me. I almost forgot what we were talking about. When he broke away, he was grinning at me like a loon. "Sex shenanigans, huh? You have stars in your eyes just from me kissing you. You love my sex shenanigans."I ground into him with my impossibly hot ass that he can't resist. If possible, he got even harder. I jumped out of his arms and off his lap. "There's no time for this nonsense!" I roared, wanting to laugh or at least smile. I never used my 'Satan voice' on him, especially not when all I wanted to do was to ride him like I was a cowgirl who rode bulls for a living. He looked shocked for a minute, but once I saw him trying to stop the corners of his lips from rising, I knew he knew I was kidding.

"Satan, I bow to you. How can I be of service to you?" he asked me as he bowed to me.

He was so hot! But not submissive! He truly didn't care that I was Satan. All that mattered to him was that he loved me, and I was his mate.

"Get up, you jerk," I said to him as I pulled him up with his tie. Hmm... his silk tie. Perhaps we would use that for a little fun later. But not right now.

We both got comfortable again, across the room from each other. The sexual tension between us filled the room. "Now help me figure out how I can convince Abaddon to let me plan Lilac's bridal shower. No one will plan the shower like I can." Now, he was no longer chuckling but laughing out loud. "Whatttttt?" I whined. Yes, Satan whined.

"Tempest, you know I love you. I would do anything for you. But your reputation for being a party planner is horrid. Demons run when they hear it suggested. There is no way in Heaven that you're going to convince Abaddon of this. Especially after he hears your suggestions. You want to have Whitney come down from Heaven to sing. Do you know how old Lilac is? Whitney is awesome, and I'd love to see her. But I'm not in my early 20s."

Evidently, Whitney Houston was too old to sing at a bridal shower. What did age have to do with it? I was as old as dirt, and I knew who Whitney was.

"Then there's the food. You want to have tacos delivered from some fast-food joint on Earth. Where did that idea come from?"

I had a reason for this one. "Lilac loves tacos, and she loves food from topside. It's a brilliant idea!" I didn't understand how he could doubt my food choice.

"Tempest, you know as well as I do Lilac will want a classy affair. Neither tacos nor fast food are classy. You sure love both, though." Okay, so he figured it out.

As much as I loved tacos and fast food, I wasn't sure they would work. Most Demons were vegetarians, but Lilac and I were not. The other Demons that lived in the castle hated it when meat was cooked because they couldn't stand the smell of it. It was Lilac's shower, so they all had to get over it. Lilac would hate a meatless bridal shower.

"Everything I do is classy, and you know it." I pouted as I sat back in his lap. "Come in, talk to Abaddon with me. Help me convince him." I could tell by his face that he was going to give in.

"You know I can't say no to you. However, I have a condition. Tell Abaddon your ideas."

Damn him! My ideas are great, but Abaddon will never agree with them. "I'll tell him my ideas," I said with my fingers crossed behind my back.

"Uncross those fingers, missy. If you don't tell him, I will." He slapped my ass hard, and that did it. I transported us to our bedroom. We'd figure out the specifics about talking to Abaddon later. Much later.

CHAPTER TWENTY-SIX

abaddon asks for permission to move topside

"ABADDON SAID he needed to speak with me as well. I wonder what that's all about. I wonder if someone told him I want to plan Lilac's bridal shower?" Jacob reached over the desk and grabbed my hand.

"Honey, you've only told me your horrible idea. Who would tell him?"

I swear to my brother God, if I didn't love this man, I would have him beheaded.

"You would not have me beheaded. You're a kind and just leader, Satan. Did you forget our mental connection, dear?"

I needed to work harder on keeping my mental blocks up around my gorgeous mate. He caught my smart-ass comments more than I liked.

"No, I did not forget that. I wanted you to hear that. Now, back to Abaddon. What did he want to talk about?"

Jacob and I looked up when we heard a knock on the door.

"Why don't you just ask me, Tempest, instead of trying to figure it out? You've been impatient since you were a little Angel. You know that's what had you jumping from Heaven, right?"

These two were annoying me already. *Maybe one little zap for each of them will make me feel better.*

"Don't you do it, Tempest. Do not zap Abaddon and me. Otherwise, I'll have to punish you later tonight." I heard Abaddon make a puking noise.

"Seriously, Jacob, I thought we were friends. I didn't need that visual in my head." That earned him a zap on his ass. "Tempest, if you zap me again, I'm zapping you back. I don't care if you are Satan. What are you going to do? Lock me in the dungeons?"

That didn't sound like a bad idea. At. All. But first, we needed to get him and Lilac married. I'd think about locking him in the dungeon after that.

"Okay, you two. I don't feel like playing the father of the Demons today. You both have something to say to each other, so why don't you tell each other what you want? Then Abaddon can tell you no, and we can move on, Tempest."

Tempest threw a shoe at me before the words were even out of my mouth. I loved my sometimes-hot-headed mate! As I ducked, they both said what they wanted. Abaddon's wish was a surprise.

"I want to plan Lilac's bridal shower!" Tempest said as she bounced on her toes.

"Lilac and I want to move topside to live in our house on Cape Cod."

Tempest slowly sank into her chair after that.

"You want to plan Lilac's bridal shower?"

"You want to move topside?"

Once again, they spoke in unison.

What did he mean by saying he wanted to move topside? What would I do without one of my closest friends and allies nearby? No, not one of my closest friends. He was as much my brother as God. And he didn't make me break out in hives like my brother.

"Abaddon, why would you want to move topside? No original

Demon has ever lived topside. You know your life will be so different up there than it is down here. I don't even know what to say to your request." Jacob came and stood by my side, tipping my head up to look at him.

"You could say yes, baby. I know Abaddon's leaving would be a significant loss, but you'll still have a lot of great guards here." He wiped the single tear that fell down my cheek. I wouldn't cry. Nope, not me. Satan didn't cry.

I looked over at Abaddon. "Before I say yes, why do you want to move topside? Also, if I say yes, I get to plan Lilac's bridal shower."

Abaddon chuckled at the last part of what I said. "As you know, the house on the Cape is where we stayed for our vacation. Lilac loved it, and honestly, after what happened with her mom, I think she needs a break from Hell. It's up to you, Tempest, of course, but please know I wouldn't ask this if I didn't think it was the best thing for my wife."

Well, that wasn't helpful. He knew I couldn't say no to a request like that.

"How about we make a deal, Abby? I'll give you permission to leave Hell for six months, and after that, if it's still what you want, I'll make a final decision. I think you're right. A break from Hell would help Lilac. She doesn't seem like herself lately. Not since you both got back from your honeymoon. Plus, I get to plan her bridal shower!"

"I did not agree with that yet, Tempest. You're a horrible party planner. Thinking about what you may plan gives me gas." Jacob shuddered. This had to be worse than I thought.

"Think of Whitney coming down from Heaven to sing, lots of pink, lots of glitter, and party games, at least one of which involves your manhood."

"Oh God, Tempest. Really?" I looked at her as she giggled.

"What? What's wrong with my plans? It will be fun! And it is only one game that involves your manhood."

I couldn't believe I was even considering this, but if it would help me get Lilac out of Hell, I'd do it. Hopefully, Lilac didn't kill me afterward!

"You can plan it, Tempest. If I have the final say on any plans that come out of that warped mind of yours." She put her hand out for me to shake.

"It's a deal. I'll plan Lilac's bridal shower, and you and Lilac can move topside for at least six months." You would think I would have known better than to make a deal with the devil after these years, but here we were.

"It's a deal."

CHAPTER TWENTY-SEVEN

almost time for the bridal shower!

IT MIGHT HAVE SEEMED like I blackmailed Abaddon to allow me to plan Lilac's bridal shower, but I would have said yes even if he had said no. He didn't have to know that, of course. Although I wanted to either send him to the dungeon ~~or behead him~~ when he said I was a horrible party planner.

I'd been organizing the shower but had told no one my plans. Every Demon working on the shower had to sign NDAs—in blood. Demons couldn't break blood contracts, no matter how many had tried. No one knew exactly what to expect tonight.

When I went down to the ballroom, I was nervous about what I would find. What if they screwed it up? It would be too late for even me to change it to the way I wanted it. I shut the door behind me because I didn't want anyone to see my masterpiece until it was time. Jacob didn't pay attention to the sign on the door that said "Keep Out by Order of Satan" because he just walked into the ballroom.

You would think my name would cause at least a little fear in those around me, but not my mate.

"What are you doing in here? Didn't you see the sign saying to keep out? That meant you, too." He had that sexy ass smirk on his face. I would love to kiss it off him, but I didn't have time for that. Whitney would arrive from Heaven soon. I had to get ready for the party.

"I saw the sign, Satan. Demons may listen to you, but I'm not a Demon. I'm not only human, but I'm also your mate." He stepped a little too close to me.

Like I said, I didn't have time. So I zapped him on his delicious ass.

"Tempest! How many times have we discussed you zapping me? This is another pair of Armani pants ruined."

"You got too close to me. I don't have time right now for sexy time, and you know I can't resist you. Now stay back." I said that last part while raising my zapping hand in the air.

"Demon, you're lucky I love you. Now, can you explain why all the colors in here are neon? And a stripper pole? This is a bridal shower, not a club. Abaddon's going to get you for this."

"The colors brighten up the place. I need to redecorate this ballroom. It's so old-looking."

Jacob pretended to cough while saying, "Bad idea."

"Jacob, I can redecorate the ballroom if I want to. None of you know what good taste is. That's why you don't like the decorations. Lilac will love it!"

"Tempest, a stripper pole."

"Jacob, bridal shower and strippers."

His eyes bulged out of his head. "When were strippers discussed? And since when do male strippers use a stripper pole?"

I started giggling. "Who said anything about male strippers, Jacob?"

He slapped his hand against his forehead. "Why didn't I realize my mate would have female strippers at a bridal shower she planned? Do you have a bunch of dollar bills for the guest of honor?"

I giggled again. "There are plenty of dollar bills for all the guests.

I hired a stripper from topside. She'll deserve all the money we can give her after stripping for a bunch of Demons."

"Okay. Is that meat I smell cooking in the kitchen? How do you think the guests will feel about the meat served during the shower? Most of you Demons can get violent when someone serves meat. I know I've said it before, but it bears repeating. You Demons are weird."

I thought about zapping him again because of that comment, but he wasn't wrong. Demons were weird. Not me, but I wasn't just any Demon. I wasn't even just an original. I was the very first Demon. "We had food sent from topside. No one will mind because Lilac loves meat, and this is her party. Is that what you're wearing? Dress up a little."

He groaned, and it almost sounded like a growl. My mate was learning a lot here in Hell. He's even decided that in the next six months, he will become a Demon. "Why did you decide we must be here, too? None of us wants to be at a bridal shower, not even Abaddon. We could have our own party."

I grabbed his hand and started walking towards the door. "That's how many people do bridal showers topside now. Now stop complaining and go get ready! I'll be up there in a few minutes to prepare myself." Before leaving, I turned around to look back at the room.

One of my closest friends was getting married and leaving Hell. Part of the reason everything was so over the top was that I hoped it would help me forget that last part. Abaddon and I had been around each other for more years than I remembered. I was going to miss him. He'd still be working here in Hell, but it wouldn't be the same with him not living here.

Before getting dressed, I went back to the kitchen to check on the food. This was going to be the party of the century. My best friend and his mate deserved no less. He and Lilac would move to their house on the Cape tomorrow morning since they wanted to move before the wedding. But before they left, we would party!

CHAPTER TWENTY-EIGHT
bridal shower

THE BALLROOM WAS FILLING UP. I invited most of the Demons in Hell to this bridal shower. Everyone loved Abaddon and Lilic—Hell, especially Lilac, so I couldn't leave Demons out. Basically, only the child Demons weren't invited.

I wanted to make sure everyone was comfortable as we party tonight, so I had Hell's main witch enhance the size of the ballroom. We couldn't have Demons all crowded into a too-small space, now, could we? That was asking for trouble, and everyone coming tonight knew they had to behave.

You see, my brother God and nephew Jesus would both be there tonight. And while Jesus was a fun guy, my brother could be a stick in the mud. Plus, I didn't want him to think he was better than me because "Angels would never act like that."

Which was total bullshit. Not only were there Angels in Heaven who should be down here in Hell, but some of them liked to party. Every party I'd been to in Heaven, which admittedly wasn't many, more than a few Angels ended up in jail for a few days.

Hopefully, they got here soon. I wanted everyone here before the guests of honor arrived. My brother liked to push my buttons, but I

SATAN, IS THAT YOU?

was sure my nephew would make sure they were here in time. Jesus was a class act. He thought he was funny, but he was not. He tried to be a comedian topside once. It was horrible. We all still laughed about that.

I was just about to go sit with Jacob at the head table when I saw them walking in. I hurried over. Not because of Bob—my brother annoys me. But because of Jesus. I adored my nephew. "Jesus, my favorite nephew. It's so great to see you. You haven't visited me in a while."

"Hi, Auntie Tempest. It's great to see you too. And I'm your only nephew." He grinned at me. He was right; he was my only nephew. "I also came down here to visit you last. It's your turn to come upstairs to visit me. My dad hired a new chef, and the food is much better."

"Jesus!" I was sure my brother was about to admonish him, but I would not let that happen.

"Bob, forget that you're God for a minute and tell me, in all honestly, that the food in Heaven doesn't suck? Or at least it used to suck. A new chef may get me up there, nephew. You know how I am about food."

Everyone knew how I was about food. It was my one addiction. Angels' and Demons' metabolisms were better than shifters.' I'd be huge if it weren't for that. I'd still be beautiful, though. Size had nothing to do with beauty.

"I have you two at the main table with Jacob and me and a few high-profile Demons. Also, Abaddon and Lilac, of course. I thought about having you in the back, Bob, but we know your ego will make you have a tantrum." The smirk on my face told my brother that I was kidding. Jesus hid his laugh behind his hand. Chicken.

As we walked to the table, the Demons at the other tables stopped Jesus from talking with him, so Bob and I walked over to our table and let him be social. Jacob stood up when we got to the table and shook my brother's hand. "God, it's great to see you. I'm glad you and Jesus could be here."

My brother looked at Jacob like he committed a cardinal sin.

"Jacob, I told you, call me Bob. You're my sister's mate. There is no reason to stand on formality with me."

Jacob looked at my brother like he had hung the sun and the moon, and I wanted to gag. I mean, he helped, but he didn't do it alone. Hell, I helped him hang the sun. I hadn't always been a Demon.

I covered my mouth as I coughed. Well, maybe not cough. Maybe pretend to cough and call my mate a kiss ass. He didn't even kiss my ass like that, and I was his mate and his ruler. Humans heard Satan and thought I was this evil creature. If they only knew.

I heard clapping before I told my mate and brother what I thought of them. I looked toward the door and saw Abaddon and Lilac walk into the room. You could see the love on their faces when they looked at each other. I'm so happy for Abaddon.

There were a few of us original Demons who recently, and finally, found our mates. Not only that, but we also saw what we were missing without them. It's an incredible feeling to find the one that Fate picked for you.

I looked over at Jacob, wondering if there was a wedding in our future. I might be Satan, but that didn't mean I wouldn't love to marry my mate. Jacob wouldn't even say the word marriage. I wasn't sure if it was because he was against it or because he wanted his proposal to be a surprise. I mentally crossed my fingers, hoping it was the latter. Satan's wedding would be huge!

CHAPTER TWENTY-NINE
there's an issue topside

WHO WAS THAT NOW? I would love to get some work done today. Jacob and I had plans to visit Abaddon and Lilac tonight. "This better be good!"

"Well, hello to you too, Tempest." Of course, it was Beatrix—my long-time vampire friend. She seemed to know when I didn't want to be disturbed.

"Beatrix, I would say it's a pleasant surprise, but I'm busy." Maybe she'd let me hang up now. Although she has no respect for my position.

"I suggest you become un-busy. We have a problem here on Earth with one, or maybe two, of your Demons, and we need you to help handle the situation. I don't think you're going to be happy."

Now, she had my attention. Few Demons lived topside, but they knew they still had strict rules to abide by if they did. They were under Hell's laws wherever they lived. That was especially important when they were topside. We couldn't have Demons acting up on Earth.

"What's going on now that I don't have time for, Beatrix? And are you sure it's one or two Demons? You know humans cause some havoc. Not to mention you vampires."

"Tempest, you know most of us vampires behave ourselves. Your Demons, though, have some issues. We know for sure there is one. A vampire in my nest just mated with a human. Well, a human-witch hybrid who never knew she was a witch."

This conversation is going off the rails. "Beatrix, what does this have to do with Demons?" I didn't have all day for this, so hopefully, she hurried up with her story.

"Grouchy today, huh?" She's pushing it today.

"Beatrix, you're getting on my nerves. Jacob and I have plans this evening, so I don't have time for this."

"I hope your plans include coming topside. You're needed. Anyway...my friend's mate's mom kept the fact that she was a witch from her three daughters. To keep this as short as possible, when that information came out, so did a lot of other information. Her mom divorced her dad."

"I'm waiting for how this involves Demons, vampire." My tone of voice this time seemed to hurry her up.

"Her dad tried to force himself into her mom's house today. He had someone with him with red skin, horns, tails, and hooves."

Now, this was a problem. He'd shown his Demon to humans. That was not acceptable at all. And to force his way into a woman's house? Nope! It looked like I'd be visiting with Beatrix tonight.

"There's more. The mom remembered some things that happened years ago and thinks her ex-husband is a Demon."

That would explain why a Demon was working with him. Demons didn't work for humans. "Name?" I needed to figure out who this was because it sounded like he never told his wife he was a Demon. That is totally against the rules.

"Howard Tate."

Oh, this wasn't good. Howard wasn't only a Demon; he was my brother. He left Hell years ago and stopped all communication with us who lived in Hell soon after. Bob hasn't heard from him since he left Hell, either. He's been gone so long that only the original Demons knew Bob and I had another sibling. He was a piece of work. If he was trying to force his way into his ex-wife's home with another Demon, no less, he was out for blood. I needed to handle this as soon as possible.

"I'll be at your house in an hour. Do you think Constantine can come with us to handle this? Howard is not only a Demon but also one we will need as much backup as possible to confront. Get Ollie and anyone else you can there, too. Howard will fight being returned to Hell, but he's coming back. He'll be no threat to your friend's mate's mother soon. Because by the end of tonight, he'll be in my dungeons."

I hung up on Beatrix to call Jacob and explained it all. I was going to need Abaddon with me as well. Beatrix ended every phone call by hanging up on the person, so that was no big deal. I knew she'd gather everyone and have them at her and Constantine's home by the time Jacob, Abaddon, and I got there. This was not the night Jacob and I had planned! Oh well, the Devil's job was never done.

CHAPTER THIRTY

family ties

JACOB and I didn't go to visit Abaddon and Lilac after all. The early evening was crazy, and once we had Howard and his Demon friend back in Hell, I just wanted to talk to Howard and go to bed with my gorgeous mate. The Devil's work was never done, and I was getting sick of it.

Seeing Howard after these years was tough. I never even knew why he left, never mind why he never returned. One thing I knew was it wasn't because of that human woman he married. He'd been gone too long, and she wasn't old enough to have been alive when he disappeared from Hell.

I heard the bedroom door open, and when I looked, I saw Jacob peeking his head in. He had hoped I would come to bed, but I didn't have time to do that right now. He opened the door a little more, and I could see by the look on his face that he was not happy with me.

"Hi, baby. I was just about to go down to the dungeons to speak with Howard. Do you want to come with me?" He wanted me to rest, which I understood. He was worried about me. Even Satan needed to rest sometimes.

The look on his face changed a little, but I couldn't tell why. "Tempest, will you go to bed as soon as you're done talking to him? I know you're the Devil, but even the Devil needs some sleep. As for whether I want to go with you, no. I'm going to go for a walk. I think you need to talk to him alone."

I knew he was right, but I didn't want to do it alone.

Jacob and I hadn't been together long, but he made me so happy and glad that I found him. Not just because he was my mate, either. It was because of him. "Yes, darling, I'll come up and go to sleep when I'm done. Thank you for always knowing what I need," I said as I walked over and kissed him before walking to the door.

Before I got to the door, he grabbed me from around my waist. "Why do I feel that this is about more than that?" It was his turn to kiss me. His kisses always melted my heart.

"Maybe because it is? As much as I would love to have you with me when I talk to Howard, I also know that we need to do this alone. You read me so well." I was being honest with him. This talk needed to be between Howard and me, even if it wasn't what I wanted.

He kissed me one more time before slapping me on my ass and pushing me to the door. "Get going. I'm ready to go to sleep, and I don't sleep well when my mate is not in bed with me."

It sounded like a line, but I knew he was telling me the truth because I felt the same way when he wasn't in bed with me.

Looking over my shoulder, I blew him a kiss and headed to the dungeons. I walked too slowly, and I knew it. But I still got to the dungeons too soon for my liking.

Ruby was sitting at the guard's desk. When she saw me walk in, she got up. She ran over to me and hugged me. "Are you okay, Tempest? I'm sure you did not have 'finding Howard' on your bingo card today."

Truer words had never been said. Honestly, I didn't think I would ever see him again.

I hugged my friend back. Ruby was an original Demon and has

been one of my best friends for years. She would know better than anyone else how this would affect me. I'd never stop being grateful for everyone who jumped from Heaven when I did. I mean, when Bob pushed me.

"I guess I'm okay. I hadn't thought about him much in years, and then suddenly, there he was. Now I must think of how I'm going to tell Bob. Is he in the last cell on the left, like I asked?" She nodded yes, and I walked down the long hall. Once I got to the end of the hall, I looked into the cell to see Howard lying on his cot, facing the wall.

I walked into the cell as quietly as possible. "Hello again, brother dear. Should I get Bob down here, and we can have a family reunion? It's been over millennia. We have so much to catch up on."

My brother looked back at me, hate in his eyes. I couldn't imagine what I had done to him to make him hate me. No matter what, I'd always loved both of my brothers. I was mad at Howard for leaving, but also happy to see him again. What was going to happen now?

In the end, I decided not to call Bob down. As soon as I finished talking to Howard, I called him to let him know the latest development down in Hell. He was as happy as I was to learn that Howard was well, but he also was nervous about his return. Howard and I had a long talk about what made him leave Hell, and it was unexpected, to say the least.

It turned out Lilith was his one true mate, and she never gave in to the mating pull. I didn't know how she was able to do that, especially now that I had met Jacob. Everyone knew that neither Bob, I, nor her husband was her one true mate. Everyone assumed she had never met him. That happened to some Demons. We had no way to know the truth since they both hid it so well.

He had to stay in the dungeons for the time being. There was no way to know how he was going to adjust to being back in Hell, and I had to be sure he never stepped foot on Earth again. He was a danger to humans, especially his family.

For now, we set up a special cell for him so he would at least be comfortable. He'd have a complete psych evaluation and regular counseling, and we would see how things go. My hope was he would be able to leave the dungeons one day, but I had to do what was best to protect everyone. Including him.

CHAPTER THIRTY-ONE

couple time

BEING the leader of Hell meant that I was very busy. Some days, I couldn't catch a minute for myself. I might be Satan, but I was still a woman with needs. Lately, my biggest need was to spend time alone with my mate.

Not having Abaddon living in Hell anymore helped nothing. Yes, he still came down to work. He was still one of my top Demons and an invaluable part of my team. But now that he and Lilac were together and living in Cape Cod, he wasn't around all the time.

I didn't regret allowing them to move topside, and they didn't know that once the six-month trial period was over, I would allow them to make their move permanent. It was just easier to handle all the issues in Hell when I had my team around all the time.

My need to have some alone time with Jacob was why I set up a date night for us. Being alone together always meant that we could be our authentic selves. There were none of the trappings that came along with me being Satan. I was Tempest, and he was Jacob. Period.

I wanted to be sure we would be completely alone, which could be difficult if we were in the castle. Even when I asked for an evening alone, if something happened, they always brought it to me. That was why I chose my cabin at the very edge of the beautiful forest. It even had a small pond where we could go skinny dipping.

I asked Abaddon to stay down in Hell tonight so we could be alone without being bothered. Lilac was coming down, too, and they were going to be staying in Abaddon's suite at the castle. Having my most trusted ally overseeing things made me feel better.

It would also give them a chance to make sure everything was okay at their home in Hell. She had been renting it out to an Angel who lived in Hell. That was rare, but it happened. The way a lot of angels behaved once they moved to Hell meant Lilac's house could be an absolute mess. Hopefully, it was fine. Abaddon and Lilac stated they would move back to Hell one day and needed the house. They both wanted to raise their children there.

Angels no longer fell from Heaven as we all did so many years ago. Now, they made an appointment to speak with God and ask for his permission, and they had to follow an entire process. Which was one reason few did it. If Demons wanted to live in Heaven, I checked with my brother to make sure it was someone he would accept in Heaven, and they were allowed to go.

Back to date night! Getting meat in Hell could be hard since a lot of Demons, me included, were vegetarians. However, Jacob was a human who was very much a carnivore. He didn't mind that he had to almost give up meat to move down here, but I liked to get him meat when I could.

Tonight, we were having his absolute favorite, steak. One of my best cooks at the castle was a chef who could cook anything, so he was making our dinner. It was going to be delicious. He'd have Demons from the kitchen bring the food down to the cabin, so it was waiting for us.

I went ahead of Jacob to ensure everything was ready for us. Just when I was about to get comfortable, Jacob arrived. He walked into the cabin with a beautiful bouquet of black roses. Satan liking black roses might be a bit of a cliché, but they truly were my favorite. They were so beautiful.

I sauntered over to him, staring into his eyes. When I got over to him, I jumped into his arms, throwing my arms around his neck and kissing him like I hadn't seen him in years. We needed this. "Hi, handsome."

We stood in the doorway, making out like human high school kids for a few minutes before we reluctantly pulled away from each other, and he put me back on the ground. "Thank you for this, Tempest. I know you have a hard time taking time off from work, but we needed some alone time. Hey! Is that steak that I smell?" His eyes lit up like a kid in a candy store.

"It is steak, a complete steak dinner with all your favorite foods. You're right; we needed this. I'm going to do a better job at making time for us. I have Demons I would trust with my life who are quite competent and can handle Hell while I take a break."

Looking back at him, I motioned to the table set with our dinner. "Let's go eat, honey." I took the flowers from his arms and brought them to the kitchen to put into a vase of water. When I was done, I brought them to the dining room and set them down in the middle of the table.

We were eating quietly, enjoying our time together, when Jacob spoke up again. "You seem tired, baby. Are you okay? Is there anything that I can do for you?"

He truly was the sweetest man, and I could hear the concern in his voice. I had given up on finding my mate after all those years, and then I found him. A human at that. No one would have guessed that Satan would have a human for a mate.

I looked at him and sighed. "It's just been a lot lately. A lot here in Hell, then finding my other brother and finding out I have three half-witch/half-Demon nieces. I'm just trying to process that. I am looking forward to the three of them coming down to visit Hell. They need to learn about their Demon heritage. I could kill Howard for doing this."

He reached over and grabbed my hands in his. "I know it's a lot, love. Especially the family issues. But you've got this. There is no one

I know who is stronger than you. And I'll be here by your side, helping all I can. Remember, you're Satan. The leader of Hell. You can handle anything."

I got up from my seat and sat on his lap. "Thank you. I know all of that somewhere in my head, but sometimes I need a reminder. Thank you for all that you do for me."

My mate then picked me up and took us to our bedroom, where we spent the rest of the night showing each other how much we loved each other.

Our lives would always be crazy. I mean, I was Satan, and craziness goes along with that. But he's right. I can get through anything. Especially with him by my side.

CHAPTER THIRTY-TWO
visiting the in-laws

IT HAD BEEN a while since I'd seen my parents, and while they loved Tempest, Hell was not their favorite place. I believed they wouldn't, or couldn't, let go of what they'd always thought Hell was like. They tried to have fun when they came to visit us, but I knew it wasn't their cup of tea.

This meant if I wanted to see my parents and wanted them to be comfortable, Tempest and I had to visit them on Earth. I had a lot of friends on Earth who didn't know who Tempest really was, so visiting my parents at home allowed me to see my friends, too.

That was what led to the two of us being at the park that afternoon when Satan made all Hell break loose on Earth. Something people who lived topside or in other realms didn't know about Tempest unless they'd spent time with her was that she was a very loving being.

But two things she would not deal with were anyone, human, Demon, vampire, anyone at all, hurting children or animals. Mostly, Tempest was even-tempered. However, if she saw a child or an animal being abused, all bets were off.

The park we went to had a walking path on which many people

walked their dogs. Trees surrounded it, and it was so peaceful. There have been rumors for years, even before anyone knew supernatural beings existed, that a witch put a spell on the park to keep it very relaxed.

No one knew if that was true or not, but on this day, walking the path was anything but relaxing. Tempest and I were casually strolling along. We had been enjoying the day and being able to spend some time alone together.

Down in Hell, we were both busy working a lot, so spending time alone together did not happen as much as we would have liked. As we were walking down the path, I saw a man walking towards us with a small dog. It looked like a Shih Tzu. Cute little pooch.

Suddenly, the dog tried to run, as dogs like to do, and the man kicked him. When I saw him kick the dog, I knew it would not be a pleasant situation. Even if I tried to stop Tempest from doing anything, I wouldn't be able to.

I glanced over at my mate and saw her horns had popped out, and her skin was a dark red. The look was complete with a tail and claws. People thought Satan had hooves, but she didn't. Like most Demons, Tempest wore a glamor most of the time. I didn't even see her true form often.

The man must have sensed the change in the air. Not surprising since Satan taking her true form created a heaviness in the air that no one could miss, especially not a human. The human gasped and tried to run. However, Tempest held him where he was with magic. Demons didn't have the same type of magic as witches; however, they had magic. It was powerful magic, too. Especially Satan's magic.

"Who...what...are you? Why can't I move? Let me go, please."

As I watched him, his pants got wet. I didn't blame him at all for being scared. If I didn't know who Tempest was, seeing her true form would scare me. Hell, even knowing Tempest, I'd be afraid if she went all Demon on me.

I walked over to Tempest, whispering so the man wouldn't hear me. "Tempest, be careful what you say here. You can't say who you are unless you want humans to know that you come topside. Maybe changing back to your glamor would be helpful."

The only acknowledgment she gave when she heard me was a tiny shake of her head. She went back to her glamor, though. I could see in her eyes what she was about to do.

"Do you want to know who I am, human? Do you think you can handle it? Because I don't think you can. But since you asked, I'll tell you. I'm the Devil. I know, not what you expected Satan to look like, blah, blah, blah. Trust me, I am Satan."

I looked from her to the man. His skin was now a gray color. Yup! He believed her. "My name is Jacob. I'm Satan's mate. There have to be many thoughts running through your head. I met Tempest when I went down to Hell for an interview. When I found out she was a female, it blew my mind. Then she told me I was her mate. It was a lot to take in."

He shook his head, maybe to show that he was listening. "You kicked your dog. Satan won't allow any abuse of animals or children. That's why she showed her Demon side. When she gets that angry, her Demon comes out."

"My dog? Oh Hell no. This mangy mutt is not my dog. I found him wandering around the park and was hoping to find his owners."

Tempest's Demon side came out again, and the man tried to take a step back. "You found this dog and wanted to help him, yet you kicked him? And your people call me evil. I've never kicked an animal in my immortal life. You're going to leave the dog with us, and we will find his owners or a suitable home. You're not going anywhere with that animal. Do you understand?"

"Whatever, I was just being nice, anyway. You two can have the hassle of finding his home." He handed the leash over to me. I wasn't sure why he even had a leash if it wasn't his dog, unless the owners lost him with his leash already connected to his collar.

Tempest let her magic go, and he almost fell on his ass. It was less than what he deserved. When he turned around and walked away, Tempest stopped him. "Give your name and address to my mate. I'll be monitoring you, so I'd be careful around animals if I were you."

The man gave me the information, and I put it in my phone with a note. Tempest will have a Demon living in this town watching him. Demons can leave Hell and live someplace else, but they always have to do Satan's bidding. She didn't take advantage of that, but it made her rest easier, knowing that there were Demons on Earth to do things if needed.

As he walked away, he started yelling that he was going to go to the tabloids about what had happened. "I don't see him doing that, Tempest. He would have nothing to gain, but people would think he was nuts. No one would believe Satan was a female unless they saw it for themselves."

Once he was gone, Tempest and I began walking again. She bent over and picked up the puppy, hugging it close to her.

"Well, I didn't have 'confront a human' on my bingo card. How about you?" I was trying to lighten the mood because I could tell that she was still furious.

"Let's go back to your mom and dad's so we can figure out what we're going to do to find his owner. If we can't find them, we'll bring him back to Hell with us. It's been ages since I've had a pet."

We walked back to my parents with Tempest holding and petting the puppy. He was adorable. I wouldn't mind having a pet at all, so I was almost hoping that we wouldn't be able to find his parents. I couldn't help myself from reaching over and petting him.

It was an exciting trip to the park, but hopefully, it wouldn't be so eventful the next time we go out.

CHAPTER THIRTY-THREE
time to go home

OUR TRIP TO visit Jacob's parents was eventful, at least on the day we found our baby. We did everything possible to find his Earth parents, but they never came forward. The feeling that the man we found him with was his actual owner never left me.

It was all okay because Jacob and I now had a pet to bring back to Hell with us. We named him Bob, after my brother. God's ego would grow knowing we named our baby after him, but it was okay. No matter how much we fought, Bob and I loved each other endlessly.

"Are you almost packed, my mate? Breakfast is ready, and my mom would love to talk over breakfast before we leave." Jumping, I turned to the door to see Jacob standing there. "I'm sorry. I didn't mean to startle you. You've been uneasy since that jerk went to the tabloids. I should be more considerate."

"No, it's fine. You were right. Telling him I was Satan was asking for trouble. Of course, he went to the tabloids."

After shutting my suitcase, I joined my mate at the door, where he wrapped his arms around me.

"Baby, we got ahead of it. So, what if people on Earth now know all about you? Most people were on your side as soon as people learned what happened, and he kicked a dog. Having that interview on the BCA news network firmly put everyone on the fence on your side. It ruined your reputation as a big, evil Demon, which I know you hate. If I'm being honest, I love it. Humans now know what I know. You're a good Demon. You're not evil."

Everything he said was right. I knew that. It was still a hard pill to swallow. The good news was Bob had come down from Heaven to do the interview with me. When he heard what happened, he insisted on being by my side.

"You must admit, their reaction to Bob was funnier than their reaction to you. Finding out in one day that Satan is not evil, and God is not perfect, melted more than a few human brains."

"Thank you for calling my brother. Having him by my side helped immeasurably. Sometimes, we act like we don't like each other, but no matter what has happened in our past, we're brother and sister and love each other very much. You're right. Everyone's reaction to Bob was hilarious. There are humans I don't think will ever recover."

We both chuckled at the thought as he wrapped me in his arms. "Having you here was also helpful; I hope you know that. You're my rock, honey. No matter what my reputation is, even the devil needs someone who has her back."

"I'll always have your back, love. We're in this life forever. Never forget that. Also, I think it's time I became a Demon, not just Satan's mate."

We hadn't discussed this topic in a long time, so his words shocked me. It was something we both knew would happen some-day. However, I didn't think it would be soon since we hadn't talked about it in a while.

"Are you sure? Becoming a Demon cannot be reversed. Once it's done, it's done. Don't you want to talk to your parents about it first? They might want to know one of their sons will no longer be human."

He had a cheeky smile on his face, which I didn't understand.

"Tempest, I talked to my parents about it right after I told them about you. Then, when all of this happened, I told them I wanted to do it soon. Like I told them, I want to protect you like you can protect me. Not only are they okay with it, but they also agree with me."

Jacob's parents were amazing. I knew that from the moment we met. This was the next level amazing, though. "Baby, I look forward to you becoming a Demon. We can complete the ceremony as soon as we get back in Hell if you'd like."

Pulling me against him with one hand, he tangled the other in my hair as he kissed me in the way only he could. We stood in his childhood bedroom, the door wide open, making out until we heard someone clear their throat behind us.

We pulled apart, and his mom and dad laughed. "Son, we have not caught you with a girl in your room in many years." His dad said to him. We both laughed, too. "I haven't been called a girl in more years than I can remember."

"No matter how old or who you are, you're still our son's mate. How about we all go for breakfast before you leave us again? I know your mom wants to spend some time with you both."

Jacob and his dad grabbed our suitcases as we left the room. Even though we had a huge wing in my castle, this room will always be my favorite place to spend time with the love of my life. It has so many memories from his childhood; I love being around it all.

CHAPTER THIRTY-FOUR
jacob proposes

BACK IN HELL...

Jacob and I returned to Hell this morning and had not had a minute alone since we stepped into the castle. Things were quiet, but Abaddon wanted to update us on everything that had happened while we were gone, and people had a million questions about the interview that my brother and I had on Earth.

That was one of the few things that my brother and I agreed on. He always agreed with me because he didn't want to ruin his reputation any more than I wanted to ruin mine. The difference was that humans had always felt he was perfect, while they'd always thought I was horrible.

I wasn't sure they were ready for the truth. Like humans, neither one of us was all good or all bad. We were more like them than they ever knew. Before the interview, Bob and I had a chat, and we agreed it was time we told the truth. We weren't too worried about the fallout from the interview. After all, I was Satan, and my brother was God. What was the worst that could happen?

When I said that to him, he looked at me as if I had lost my mind. Maybe I had. It wasn't that I thought nothing bad could happen because of our revelation—it was that I felt we were God and Satan. What could anyone do to us? Luckily, we never found out. Jacob, Bob, and I stayed on Earth for an extra week to make sure everything was fine. And it was. Humans took it well.

Of course, some people proclaimed that my brother and I being on earth together signaled the end of days. Those people still swore that the earth was going to blow up or something, that human life was going to cease to exist. We didn't tell them we had already been on Earth together many times.

After what seemed like an eternity, Jacob and I were back in our wing of the castle. I was ready to fall into bed, but Jacob had other ideas.

"Honey, I planned a dinner in the formal dining room, just for us. You don't mind, do you?"

I didn't mind, exactly. It was just that I wanted to take a shower and relax in bed. "You don't want to rest tonight? It's been a long day for both of us. I would love a shower and bed. And is the formal dining room just for us? We don't need to have dinner in the formal dining room. We can have whatever you planned sent up to us. I'm sure no one would mind."

He looked at me with a strange smile on his face, and his eyes all lit up like a kid at Christmas. How could I say no to him? "You know what? Sure! Let's do it. If we can make it an early night."

He pulled me up from where I was sitting on the bed and took me in his arms, holding me tight. "We'll make it an early night, baby. I promise. Well, I promise we'll be back up here early." He winked at me. Suddenly, I was wide awake.

We both wanted to get back up to our rooms sooner rather than later. We had been on Earth at Jacob's parents' house for far too long. Although we shared the bed at their house, neither of us wanted to have sex with them right down the hall. I needed to show my mate how much I loved him.

When we got to the formal dining room, I noticed they had replaced the normal large table that seated thirty with a much smaller table set for two in the middle of the room. Also, a violinist playing a few feet from the table.

I turned to Jacob, amazed that he had arranged all of this. "What's this for, my love? What did I do to deserve this?" I couldn't stop the smile that claimed my face or the tears streaming down my face. My mate was so sweet when he wanted to be, but we were both always so busy that we rarely had time to plan dates like this.

He took my face in his hands and gave me the softest kiss before responding. "I would do anything for you, my angel. You deserve this and so much more." He took one of my hands in his, and we walked towards the table.

"Did you just call me an Angel?" I asked, chuckling. With the room so empty, all sounds seemed to echo. Calling Satan an angel didn't sound right to me at all.

He stopped walking and pulled me to him. "Sweetheart, before you were ever Satan, you were an Angel. Don't you ever forget that. You had your reasons for jumping from Heaven. Although you can't change the fact that you jumped, you also can't change the fact that you began your life as an Angel. And to me, you'll always be an Angel. Now, let's go have our dinner so we can get back to our wing."

We were having a fantastic dinner when Jacob suddenly stood up and took something out of his pocket. He did a great job hiding it, but I knew what it was as soon as he got down on one knee. I gasped, and tears fell down my face once again. I was supposed to be the baddest creature out there, but this man still could bring tears to my eyes.

When he looked up at me, I saw he was weeping as well. No matter what happened, I could never deny how much my mate loved me. I'd never know how I got so lucky when I met him, but Satan had done something right.

"Tempest, I've never met a woman like you. A woman who makes my heart swell to at least twice its size just by looking at you. I've never known a love like the one I have with you, and I know that with everything in me, I would never have a love like this with any other woman. I not only want to spend the rest of my life with you, but I also want to spend the rest of my life as your husband. Will you marry me?"

I jumped up from my seat and into his arms, knocking him to the floor. Without moving, I put my hand out to him. "It would make me the happiest Demon in the world, in any realm, to be your wife, Jacob. You've brought so much joy into my life. I couldn't imagine loving anyone as much as I love you."

He placed the ring on my finger and sat up. Before pulling us both up off the floor, he kissed me like we were reuniting after years of being apart. I gave him as good as he gave me.

After all the many, many years that I've been around, I finally found my happily ever after. Jacob and I may not be a traditional couple, but we have a love that will last for all eternity. Which is good, since once Jacob becomes a Demon, we will both live for all eternity.

The end... for now!!

Tempest and Jacob will return. Questions will be answered. The biggest wedding ever held in Hell will happen. I hope you return to Hell with me when Book 2 is released!

about the author

Janet Lee Smith, a nearly 60-year-old native of New Bedford, MA, harbored a decade-long aspiration to become an author. Despite repeatedly delaying this dream, she finally took decisive action at 51, putting an end to procrastination and transforming her writing aspirations into reality. Celebrating 15 years of marital bliss with her wife, Shanna, Janet has shared her life with Shanna for over two decades. Their home is a lively abode, housing their playful canine companion, Daime, and their dignified feline friend, Star. Janet and Shanna cherish the unique dynamics of their household.

other works by janet lee smith

Falling In Love

All of My Kindle Vella Stories

.